A CHRISTMAS IN THE ALPS

A CHRISTMAS IN THE ALPS

MELODY CARLSON

THORNDIKE PRESS
A part of Gale, a Cengage Company

LIBRARY OF CONGRESS CIP DATA ON FILE.
CATALOGUING IN PUBLICATION FOR THIS BOOK
IS AVAILABLE FROM THE LIBRARY OF CONGRESS.

ISBN-13: 978-1-4328-9083-4 (hardcover alk. paper)

Published in 2021 by arrangement with Revell Books, a division of Baker Publishing Group.

Printed in Mexico
Print Number: 01   Print Year: 2022

A Christmas in the Alps

CHAPTER 1

Simone Winthrop knew all about loss. But as she sorted through her dead grandmother's cluttered house, she experienced an unexpected wave of hopefulness. Because, really, what was left to lose? Sure, it was a backward way to view life, but it helped on days like today.

"Hey, Simone," Andrea Jacobs called from what used to be a pleasant guest room but over the years had morphed into a space that could be featured in an episode of *Hoarders.* Simone had meant to clear it out when she'd moved back here to help Grandma Betty, but with the responsibilities of caring for her ailing grandmother these past couple of years . . . somehow she'd just never gotten around to it.

"Come look at this," Andrea called out again.

"What is it this time?" Using her foot to push aside the half-filled box of old pottery,

Simone shoved a loose auburn tendril beneath the old bandana she'd tied on to keep the dust out. She picked her way through the living room maze of cardboard boxes, plastic packing crates, and just plain trash. It'd seemed a good idea to have her childhood best friend lend a hand with clearing out the house, but she now realized how easily Andrea got distracted with odd bits and pieces. Particularly family memorabilia.

"Unless you've unearthed the original Declaration of Independence or the crown jewels, I'm not sure I'm interested." Simone smirked as she leaned against the doorframe. "What's up?"

Andrea frowned. "Seriously, Simone, you should be more grateful. Without me here, you'd probably have thrown some important stuff away." She pointed to a box she'd been using to store items she felt needed preservation. "What about your great-grandpa's war medals and those photos of him in his military uniform?" She picked up the old wedding photo of him and his war bride and held it up. "I still can't believe how much you look like your great-grandmother." She pointed to the young Simone Sophia — Simone's namesake — and smiled. "I wish this photo was in color.

I'll bet her hair was auburn like yours."

"As a matter of fact, it was. But I've seen that photo a million times." Simone bent down to pick up an old needlework pillow she remembered from childhood. "I guess I'll keep this." She shook off the dust then tucked it under her arm. "Okay, what's so important that —"

"This letter." Andrea held up what looked like a perfectly normal envelope. "It's never been opened."

"Well, that's nothing. Grandma Betty was always forgetting things. I found a grocery sack stuffed with unopened mail and bills when I first came to help out."

"Yeah, I know. But this letter is addressed to *you*, Simone. And the return address is *Mrs. Simone Sophia Winthrop.* Isn't that your great-grandmother?"

"Yeah." Simone made her way through the messy room. "But she passed away more than two years ago."

"Maybe so, but this postmark is nearly three years old."

Simone took the thin envelope from Andrea, curiously studying the lacy handwriting. "This was mailed from the assisted-living center that Great-grandmamma went into after Great-grandpapa died." Simone read the postmark. "You're right about this

9

date. It seems to have been written a few months before she died."

"Maybe it's a check, Simone. Your inheritance. Wouldn't that be cool?"

"Great-grandmamma wasn't wealthy."

"What about that cool house she had in San Francisco? I remember when I went with you to visit her. That must've been worth a bundle."

"Except they got a reverse mortgage on it when my great-grandfather needed care." Simone flipped the envelope over to see it was still securely sealed. "It's never been opened."

"I know. Why didn't Grandma Betty give you this letter?"

"Just one more sign of her early-onset Alzheimer's. I noticed some memory issues with her when I was in college, but I assumed she was grieving for Grandpa. Then it kept getting worse. When a neighbor called saying she'd walked down the street in her nightgown, calling for a dog that had been gone for years, I knew we had a problem."

"Yeah, I have an uncle with Alzheimer's. It's sad." Andrea tapped the envelope. "Anyway, don't you want to see what's inside?"

Simone used her fingernail to carefully slit

open the top of the envelope. "At least Great-grandmamma had all her marbles up until the end. You know, she was ninety-three when she died."

"Hopefully you got her genes." Andrea moved closer as Simone slid out the slim one-page letter. "What's it say?"

Simone took in a deep breath then began to read aloud. As she read, she could almost hear Great-grandmamma's sweet French accent.

My dearest Simone Sophia,

I am a very old woman who has lived a very good life. I married a good man, and I miss him dearly. Time is soon when we will meet again. But this is not why I write to you today, dearest great-granddaughter. I have an important message for you. I sent it to your grand-mother, my daughter-in-law, last spring. But I do not hear back from her, so I am worried you will not know.

I asked Betty to tell you about my treasure —

"Her *treasure*!" Andrea interrupted. "So this really is a valuable letter?"

"I don't know." Simone frowned. "Maybe I'm wrong. Maybe Great-grandmamma was getting loopy too."

"Go on. Keep reading," Andrea urged her.

Simone returned her focus to the letter, continuing where she left off.

My treasure stayed behind when I left France. I hid it in a secret place. I tried to send for it many years ago, but life grew busy. I forgot and my treasure seemed lost to me. But now, I remember my treasure. It haunts me like an old melody. More than anything in life, I want to share my treasure with you, Simone Sophia. It is for you and only you, ma chérie. If I were not so ancient and worn out, I would go there and bring it back for you. But I cannot.

My treasure is hidden in Avre —

"In an oven?" Andrea interrupted again.

"No, not an oven. *Avre* is in France. It's spelled A-V-R-E but my great-grandmother pronounced it more like *ov-eh.* Her family home was there. I actually wrote a research paper on Avre in middle school. All I remember is that it's this really small town in the French Alps and that it burned to the ground in the 1800s. Great-grandmamma never spoke of it much, but I know it's where she met my great-grandpapa during

World War II. I remember asking her if she ever missed her family, or wanted to go back, but she didn't seem to care. I almost got the feeling something went wrong back —"

"Never mind all that, Simone. I want to hear about the treasure. Keep reading!"

"Then stop interrupting." Simone felt her hands tremble slightly as she held up the letter and continued to read.

My treasure is hidden in Avre. I know it must still be there. You must go and get it, ma chérie. It is meant for you. For you alone. Please, waste no time. Go and get it, Simone Sophia. My treasure will be your treasure. If I know you have secured it, I can die a happy woman.

All my love, ma chérie,
Simone Sophia Beaumont Winthrop

"I knew this letter was important," Andrea declared. "I could just feel it. What do you think the treasure could be? Money? Gold? The deed to the family home? Maybe your great-grandmother's family was wealthy."

Simone ignored her as she reread the letter, trying to grasp the meaning.

"You could be rich, Simone." Andrea grabbed her by the arm, giving her a shake. "Think about it, this could be something really big. Aren't you just a tiny bit excited?"

Simone blinked then slowly nodded. "Yes, of course, it's exciting. But think about it, Andrea. Great-grandmamma Simone left during World War II. She hadn't been in France for . . . well, decades."

"Yes, but she sounded pretty certain that her treasure was safely hidden in Avre. It must still be there. Maybe it's in her childhood home. Don't people in France keep homes in the family for generations?"

"Even if she hid it in her family home, what are the chances it hasn't been found by someone? Or that her relatives still live in the same house? And even if her mysterious treasure is still there, how could I possibly find it? How would I know where to look?"

"Stop being so negative. Just imagine if you did find it — how cool would that be? It would give you an even stronger connection to your namesake. She was such a cool lady. You need to do this."

"Get real, Andrea. Even if I miraculously found this supposed treasure that probably doesn't even exist, how could I prove to anyone that it was mine?"

"The letter." Andrea pointed to the page still in Simone's hand. "That's your proof."

"But, honestly, I wouldn't know where to begin." Furthermore, Simone had no desire to board a jet and fly clear to France. Not that she planned to admit her deep-rooted flying fears to Andrea.

"Oh, Simone, this is an adventure just waiting for you. Weren't you just telling me you were ready for some sort of big change in your life?"

Simone did recall saying something to that effect last night. But only after Andrea had insisted on opening an old bottle of wine she'd found buried in the back of the pantry. After a couple of sips of what tasted more like vinegar then wine, Simone had confessed that she did want something more.

"I only meant that I didn't plan to go back to being a dental assistant," she said. "I'm done with that."

"And I'm glad you are. I've always known that you were meant for something bigger and better than cleaning teeth."

Simone felt defensive. "There's nothing wrong with being a dental assistant. Grandma Betty was one — and that's how she met Grandpa Hal."

"Yeah, yeah — I know the drill. You were

supposed to marry a dentist like Betty did and live happily ever after." Andrea rolled her eyes. "So, how's that working for you, girlfriend?"

Simone just laughed it off as she slid the letter into her sweatshirt pocket. It wasn't that she hadn't had an opportunity to marry a dentist, but after several years of dating one, she realized that was not *her* dream. Jonathan was nice enough — but he was boring. Grandma Betty's deteriorating health had provided Simone the perfect excuse to bid Jonathan adieu. No regrets.

"You've always been a creative spirit." Andrea's words nudged her back to the present. "Remember high school and those first college years . . . how you loved art and dance and theater? You had dreams, Simone."

"Maybe. But then Grandpa Hal died. And, well, it was like my wake-up call."

"To grow up and start adulting? You weren't even twenty-one."

"Grandma Betty needed my support —"

"Yeah, yeah, I know. But she doesn't need you now. And from what I can see, you're free to do whatever you like." Andrea checked her phone. "Unlike me. Looks like Mom's ready for me to pick up the girls. Olive and Macy get a little crazy around this time of day. That's why they call it the witching hour."

"Well, thanks for helping today. And thank your mom too. Give your little angels a hug from me."

Andrea took a couple of minutes to explain which boxes were destined for the dumpster and which ones could go to the storage unit Simone had rented. "And I'll come back again on Saturday. Jerrod promised a daddy day with the girls so I can help you some more." She glanced around the living room. "It might seem overwhelming right now, but we're closer than it looks."

"I hope you're right." Simone wasn't convinced.

"And when I come on Saturday, we're going to start making plans for you to take a little trip to France."

Simone grimaced. "We'll see."

"I just wish I could go with you."

"Now, that might be fun." Simone opened the front door to see that dark clouds had already rolled in. "Looks like that rainstorm's about to let loose."

"Better get those buckets lined up," Andrea said, teasing.

"Just *one* bucket," Simone reminded her. "The roof only leaks in the laundry room. And I have a roofer scheduled to come check it out right after Thanksgiving."

"That's more than a week away. Sure you won't be under water by then?"

Simone shrugged. "It is what it is." She picked up the box she'd filled with odds and ends she thought Olive and Macy might enjoy. "Don't forget this."

"Thanks. The girls are going to love it." Andrea pulled on the hood of her jacket just as the sky opened up and started to pour. "Maybe you should just skip the roofer and sell the house as is. Even with a leaky roof, you'd get a good price. I heard it's still a seller's market. Then you'd be free to go treasure hunting in France!"

"You're like a dog with a bone." Simone laughed.

"A really nice bone. Think about it, Simone. A French Christmas!" Andrea sighed dreamily. "Isn't that tempting? *Christmas in the French Alps?* And after you find your treasure, you can come home a rich woman."

Simone smiled as she shook her head. "You are totally delusional!"

"Excuse me for having an optimistic imagination!" Andrea waved and dodged raindrops as she dashed out to her minivan.

Standing on the front porch, Simone watched the fat raindrops splatting down on the cement footpath. Hopefully she was right about the leak being limited to the laundry room roof. It was the first big rain since last spring and looked to be a real deluge. As raindrops morphed into sheets of water, Simone remembered one of Grandma Betty's favorite songs — "It Never Rains in Southern California." Hadn't she just packed the Albert Hammond record in one of the "To be saved" boxes? Maybe she'd dredge it out and fire up her grandma's old stereo this evening. Just for old times' sake.

She sighed as she closed the front door against the Southern California rainstorm, wondering — not for the first time — if she really wanted to continue living here. There was so much she didn't like about this region . . . the weather, the traffic, the earthquakes.

And what about the loneliness during the holidays? Andrea's words echoed through her head — *Christmas in the French Alps.* Of course, it sounded absolutely wonderful. Like a beautiful dream. But Simone knew from experience, dreams like that didn't come true. Not for her anyway. *C'est impossible.*

CHAPTER 2

By the time Andrea returned to help on Saturday morning, Simone had made good progress on sorting and packing. "I'm not saying I don't need you," Simone confessed as Andrea handed her a Starbucks cup, "but I think the end's in sight."

"Well, we don't have to tell Jerrod we're slackers today. I wouldn't want to spoil his daddy day with the girls." Andrea chuckled as she removed a partially packed box from a kitchen chair and sat down.

"Okay, I do appreciate you being here for me." Simone cleared a spot on the table. "Packing up a dead woman's belongings gets a little depressing. Not to mention lonely."

"For sure." Andrea tore open the brown bag she'd brought, revealing a small assortment of baked goods. "That was quite a rainstorm. How's the roof holding up?"

"Still just leaking in the laundry room.

One of the leaks goes straight into the washing machine. But I had to empty the bucket a few times." Simone broke a croissant in half.

"Thinking about my suggestion?" Andrea reached for a cinnamon roll.

"Which suggestion?" Simone dodged the question, knowing full well what Andrea was talking about.

"To sell your house and go to France, silly girl."

Simone laughed as she chewed on a bite of croissant. "You make it sound so simple."

"It is simple. You just make up your mind and do it. And, seriously, what about that treasure? I was thinking about it last night. Don't you want to find out what your great-grandmother left you?"

Simone rolled her eyes. "I seriously doubt it even exists. The more times I read her letter, the crazier it all sounds. She was old, Andrea. And she missed Great-grandpapa. It's possible she grew a bit senile toward the end. It happens."

"You said yourself that she'd always been sharp as a tack. And why of all things would she imagine a hidden treasure?"

"I don't know . . . but even if it were real, do you honestly think a nearly eighty-year-old treasure would still be wherever it was that she put it? It's totally absurd."

"Who cares if it's absurd?" asked Andrea. "It would be an adventure. And you need an adventure. Plus, you'd be in France, Simone! Wouldn't that be fabulous? Can you imagine?"

"You're such a dreamer."

"You could do this. Seriously, what's to stop you? You've always had to put your dreams on hold. But not now. You're not tied to a job and you've got enough in your savings to cover the trip."

"Drain my savings for a crazy trip to France?"

"You'll have money from selling this house, which I wanted to —"

"Traveling to France? In the wintertime? I don't know." Simone didn't intend to admit to her crazy fears or that the mere thought of stepping onto a plane made her feel sick to her stomach.

"But it would be the French Alps. They're beautiful in winter. I actually googled Avre, and it's this perfectly charming old-world town. It reminded me of the village my mom puts under her Christmas tree every year. Only it's real."

Simone nodded somberly. "I know . . . I actually googled it last night too."

"So, aren't you dying to go there? I mean

it's your ancestors' home. Wouldn't you love to see it in person?"

"Of course, I'd love to see it, but I —"

"Listen to me, Simone," Andrea said, cutting her off. "I've been giving this a lot of thought. I decided that you — of all people — deserve it."

Simone sighed. "Deserve it?"

"Mom and I were talking about it the other day. She reminded me of a few things. You know, about your life."

"What about my life?" Simone frowned.

"Well, I don't want to drag you through the past, but you've had some pretty hard breaks. I mean, for starters — your mom. Not everyone gets abandoned and left with their grandparents."

Simone felt a lump in her throat. "My grandparents loved me more than —"

"Yes, yes, I know. But your mom just disappears and never comes back. Then you don't even know who your dad is. You're barely out of high school and your grandpa dies tragically, so you put your life on hold and spend the next couple of years helping your grandma get over the loss. When you finally go to college, it's not for anything that truly interests you. No, you let Betty talk you into taking the safe route."

"It seemed sensible at that time," Simone

said defensively.

"Yeah, yeah. But then Betty gets Alzheimer's, and you give up your job — your *boring* job — to come back here to help her. You deserve *more,* Simone, and Mom and I decided that your great-grandmother and Betty are now your ticket to getting it. Voilà!"

"How so?" Simone tried to appear nonchalant as she sipped her latte.

"Betty left you this house so you have plenty of money, and your great-grandmother left you some hidden treasure to motivate you to go. Call it fate or kismet or God directing your path, but the implications are obvious. You are meant to go to France."

"Wow, you've obviously given this some thought." Simone felt slightly amused . . . and touched. "Thanks, but no —"

"No more buts!" Andrea set her coffee cup down so hard that it splashed over the side. "You *have* to go. If nothing else, do it for me. I'll live vicariously through you. I've always wanted to go to France. And the French Alps at Christmas? How can you possibly say no?"

Simone sighed, looking over to the kitchen cupboards. "I still have the kitchen to pack and —"

"Simone Sophia Winthrop, are you even listening to me?"

"Yes, of course. And I can't deny that visiting France does sound lovely. It's just that I have so much to do still, and I —"

"Okay, then, think about this." Andrea locked eyes with her. *Family.*

"Family?"

"Yes. Family." Andrea tilted her head to one side. "Where's yours?"

Simone felt a lump in her throat as she considered this. "Dead . . . and gone."

"That's right. I didn't want to drag you down, but you don't have one single living relative, do you? None that you know of anyway. But you *might* have some family members in France. Go look up the Beaumonts of Avre."

Simone smiled. "I don't know why you quit law school, Andrea. You'd have made a great attorney."

"Thanks." Andrea looked smug. "I do plan to finish law school when the girls are a little older."

"Okay, I'm considering what you said, and it's very tempting." Simone took a slow sip of coffee, trying to decide how much she wanted to disclose about her flying fear.

"Well, let's make it even more tempting." Andrea leaned forward with a twinkle in her eye. "Mom and I think we've found a buyer for your house."

"Seriously?"

"Yep, and we won't even charge you a realtor commission."

"Who?" Simone set down her cup.

"My brother. Mom told Brandon you're getting ready to sell, and he's been dying to move back to the old neighborhood."

"Brandon and Leslie in *this* house? Does he know the shape it's in?"

"Brandon's handy. The boy can sling a hammer. Anyway, they'll be here for Thanksgiving. How about if he and Leslie come check it out?"

"That's fine." Simone grimaced. "But once they see the laundry room leak, they'll probably run the other way."

"Oh, come on, Eeyore, why don't you let them figure that out?"

"Eeyore?" Simone couldn't help but laugh.

"Well, that's who you remind me of. I was just reading *Winnie the Pooh* to the girls, and Eeyore is so glum, always looking for the negatives."

"Okay then." Simone stood with fresh determination. "I think that I *positively* need to get to work if I only have five days to get

26

this place looking good for Brandon and Leslie."

"That's the spirit. The sooner you sell this house, the sooner you go to France."

Simone just laughed. Maybe Andrea had it right . . . maybe a trip to the French Alps was possible. As they continued to sift and sort and pack, she tried to imagine being in France. Sure, she'd love to do it, and to see Avre . . . but flying? The thought of a plane made her heart pound and palms sweat. Maybe she could travel by ship. Did people still do that?

If anyone had told Simone she'd sell Grandma Betty's house by Thanksgiving, she'd never have believed them. But when Brandon and Leslie made a fair-priced cash offer for her "as is" house, she gladly accepted. They shook hands on it and by Monday, the stunningly huge check was deposited into her bank account. Two days later, Simone found herself parked in Andrea's spare room, wondering what to do next.

Of course, Andrea now claimed Simone had no excuse for not making the trip to France. No reason not to go seek out her treasure. And on Wednesday night, Andrea insisted on helping Simone book her flight.

"It's super easy," she told Simone as she opened her laptop on the kitchen island. "I arrange trips for Jerrod all the time, and Wednesday is always the best day to book. All I need is your credit card."

"But I'm not absolutely certain I want to go," Simone protested.

"Of course you want to go. You *have* to go." Andrea beamed at her. "And I know your passport's good because you got it before we drove to Mexico for my thirty-fifth birthday last summer." She pointed to the screen. "See, I already got the ticket started for you. A direct flight from LAX to CDG."

"What does that even mean?" Simone asked.

"It means you don't change planes between LA and Charles de Gaulle airport in Paris. It's a nonstop flight. Cool, huh?"

"Oh?" Simone's eyes widened. "How long would I be on that plane?"

"Around eleven hours. You'll leave at 3:20 p.m. and arrive at 11:10 a.m. Isn't this exciting?"

"Yeah . . . exciting." Simone could hear the flat tone in her voice. "Andrea, there's a problem."

"What?" Andrea continued to fill in Simone's travel information.

"I'm scared of flying."

Andrea looked up. "Serious?"

"Dead serious." She barely nodded. "Remember how Grandpa Hal died?"

"But that was a small, private plane." Andrea's brows arched. "And it was a freak accident."

Simone shrugged. "The point is, he didn't survive."

"Yes, but that almost never happens with big commuter jets. It's more dangerous to drive a car than fly in a plane — and you do that all the time. Even riding a bicycle is more dangerous than flying. You can't really be *that* scared."

"Yes, I can. And I am." Simone bit her lip.

"But you can get over it. The way to get past your fears is to face them. Do you realize how freeing it will be for you to conquer this?"

Simone shook her head sadly.

Andrea reached for her hand, squeezing it as if to impart strength. "You can do this, Simone. You're one of the bravest women I know. The way you helped Betty after your grandpa died and the way you hung in there with her through her Alzheimer's . . . only a very courageous woman could've done that. You're no coward."

"Except when it comes to planes and flying."

"Which is exactly why you need to do this." Andrea held up her forefinger. "And there's another reason too. Remember the end of your great-grandma's letter? She said she would only die happy if she knew you'd gotten the treasure."

"But she's dead."

"Maybe she's up there watching you. You could be making her unhappy right now. Just because you're too scared to go get that treasure."

Simone rolled her eyes. "You mean a treasure that probably doesn't exist."

"You don't know that." Andrea turned back to the computer. "Go get your credit card, and then come back and answer these questions for me."

Although Simone handed over her card and pretended to cooperate, she couldn't imagine boarding a plane . . . let alone flying! But she kept her thoughts to herself as Andrea busily typed information into the laptop.

"I just don't think I can do this," Simone finally burst out. "I mean for my first flight — being stuck in a plane for so long. Even if I got over my fears, I'd probably get claustrophobic and pass out."

"Great. Everyone will just assume you're sleeping."

"What if I totally lose it somewhere over the Atlantic Ocean? What if I stand up and scream and freak everyone out? Eleven hours on a plane? It's just too much."

"Okay, so let's not book a direct flight." Andrea tapped something new into her keyboard. "I saw a great deal that connects in Seattle. The flight up there is only two and a half hours. That could be a good first flight for you. Short and sweet."

"I don't know." Simone imagined herself tumbling off the plane in Seattle and never getting on another flight — ever.

"Hey, this is lots cheaper too. Plus, you'll have a little layover in Seattle. You can walk around, get your bearings, and grab something to eat." Andrea continued to chatter cheerfully as she changed the arrangements. Before long, the flights were actually booked. "Just think, Simone, ten days from now, you'll be in Paris."

Simone wasn't so sure about that, but since her friend was not taking no for an answer, she just nodded again. What would be would be . . . and perhaps none of this would ever actually be. No one could force her to board a plane!

"Now, I'm sure you'll want a couple of

days in Paris. You arrive on Friday so you might as well stay through the weekend. Oh, Simone — Paris during the Christmas season. It'll be magical." Soon she was booking three nights in a Parisian hotel and then arranging train transportation to Avre on the following Monday morning. "It's a long train ride. Looks like five to eight hours, depending on the time of day. You're not afraid of trains, are you?"

"No, of course not."

"I'm sure it'll be a pretty trip. You'll see a lot of French countryside."

"That sounds nice." If only she could take a train from LA to France!

"And look at this." Andrea pointed to a photo of an old-fashioned building. "You could stay here in Avre. It's called Château Edelweiss, and it's got high customer ratings. Isn't it perfectly adorable?"

As Simone studied the pictures of Avre and the hotel, she almost relaxed. "It does look charming."

"Great. We'll book you through Christmas. Of course, you could always switch accommodations if you find something better. Or if your relatives want you to stay with them. Wouldn't that be fun?"

Simone couldn't imagine having French relatives, let alone being a guest in their home, but she never would've imagined any of this just a week ago. She felt like her brain was about to explode. And yet, at the same time, she felt excited. She was really doing this!

"So, we're all set." Andrea handed the credit card back. "Good thing you're so rich, girlfriend. For all we know, you'll be even richer when you come home. I wouldn't mind having an heiress for my best friend."

"Don't hold your breath." Simone stood, pocketing her credit card as she thanked Andrea for her help. Okay, it did feel slightly intrusive, but she knew her friend meant well. Besides, Simone told herself as she returned to her room, she could cancel the whole trip if she wanted. Sure, Andrea would probably throw a fit and disown her, but it was a comfort to know she could pull the plug if necessary. And, short of a miracle, it would be necessary. But a miracle would be much nicer!

CHAPTER 3

On Friday afternoon, Andrea presented Simone with a workbook. "Jerrod picked this up for you as a thank-you for babysitting the girls tonight."

"Soar Above the Fear of Flying." Simone laughed, reading the cover. "Clever concept."

"He said it's highly recommended. A work associate swears it changed her life."

"You honestly think *this* will help?" She waved the flimsy booklet in the air.

"Well, it can't hurt. I took a peek. Some of the exercises seemed well thought out. Just promise you'll try it, okay?"

"I'll give it a look after I get your girls to bed."

"And good news." Andrea grinned. "Jerrod agreed to another daddy day tomorrow."

"That's nice. Big plans?"

"Yes. You and I are going clothes shopping."

"Clothes shopping?" Simone frowned. "I already have too much crammed into your spare room as is. In fact, I was just bagging things to donate."

"That's great. You should donate all of it. Hopefully Goodwill won't reject it."

"Thanks a lot."

Andrea laughed. "Hey, you have to admit your wardrobe's gotten pretty sad."

"Well, my work clothes were practical. And it's not like I dressed to impress while caring for Grandma." But Simone knew Andrea was right — her wardrobe was pretty pathetic.

"Yeah, I noticed." Andrea frowned at Simone's basic outfit of worn jeans and a torn sweatshirt, then patted her back. "High time you stepped it up, girlfriend."

"Hey, these are babysitting clothes."

"Babysitting, caregiving, house-packing, you name it. Those are the only kinds of clothes I ever see you in anymore. It's depressing."

"You're probably right." Simone smiled sheepishly. "I'm in a rut."

"Well, since I plan to live vicariously through you — I mean, on your trip to France — I want us to do it with class.

Tomorrow we're getting some stylish clothes and respectable luggage. We will do this thing in style."

On Saturday Simone attempted to "step it up" by wearing a hand-knit sweater and a newer pair of jeans. But compared to Andrea, who'd actually donned a stylish skirt and jacket plus fashionable boots, Simone felt drab. She really did want to make a change.

"I thought we'd start here." Andrea drove her minivan into an upscale mall that Simone had never even seen before.

"Looks kinda spendy." Simone read the designer names on the store signs. Not labels she'd ever bought — or wanted to.

"Hey, you can afford it." Andrea pointed to a store as she parked nearby. "I really like this place. In fact, I asked Jerrod to get me a gift certificate here for Christmas."

"I don't know." Simone studied the sleek window display. "It seems a little pedestrian to me."

"Pedestrian?" Andrea turned to stare at her as she shut off the ignition.

"You know, everyday, uninspired, ho-hum." Simone pointed to the storefront. "That outfit looks like something a corporate executive might wear to work. Too stiff and conventional for me."

Andrea laughed as they got out of the minivan. "Well, didn't you suddenly turn into the little fashion critic."

"Hey, I'm going to France. You said I should go in style."

"Absolutely. So what do you have in mind?"

"To be honest, I'm not even sure what I like anymore," she said as they stepped inside. "I mean, I loved boho chic back in high school. But I guess that's not really trending right now."

"I don't know about trending, but if you ask me, anything goes with fashion. Now that you mention it, you did like artsy clothes growing up. I've always been more into traditional styles, but with your height and that head of auburn hair, you can pull off drama. You're so right, this store is totally not you." Andrea paused to look around. "But I know some shops you might like — just a couple of miles from here. They're kind of unconventional and free-spirited."

"Don't get me wrong, I'm not saying I want to look like a gypsy or a hippie," Simone said as they got back in the van. "I just don't want to look like a legal secretary."

"I get that. You should wear clothes that

express your personality and make you feel good." Andrea frowned at Simone's lackluster outfit. "And sorry, sweetie, but that's not cutting it."

The next selection of shops looked more promising. After browsing through a couple of shops that were close but not quite right, Simone discovered a boutique that seemed to speak her language. It was even called Bonjour! The interesting shop had an amazing selection of both new and vintage clothes — everything from unique shoes to big, floppy hats. Before long, Simone was trying on flowing skirts and interesting belts and colorful scarves. A young salesgirl named Clive really got into the spirit of things, bringing Simone item after item, helping her to put together fun outfits with personality and flare.

"Now, this just makes me happy," Simone told Andrea and Clive as she stood in front of the big mirror outside the dressing room. She wore a vintage lacy top, cinched in with a thick woven belt, over a longish tapestry skirt, topped with an oversized cardigan and set off by a pair of really cool boots.

"And you could switch out the skirt for jeans if you want," Clive told her.

"Or add a scarf." Andrea slung a paisley scarf around Simone's neck. "This one really looks great with your green eyes."

Simone tried to peek at the price tag, but for the umpteenth time, Andrea stopped her. "For once in your life, could you just not worry about the cost? You can afford it, Simone. And you deserve it."

Before she could protest, Andrea took the scarf and put it on the growing pile of "must-haves."

"I don't want to get too much," Simone reminded them. "I know there are limits to what you can carry on a plane."

"Don't worry, you'll be checking a bag," Andrea assured her. "Which reminds me, we still need to find you some luggage."

"You should check out Matilda's," Clive told Simone. "It's a few stores down. They have some really cool travel pieces that I think you'd like."

By midafternoon, both Simone and Andrea were over shopping. "We really did shop till we dropped," Andrea said as they piled bags and boxes in the back of her minivan. "But you're definitely set for your trip now."

"My trip," Simone muttered as she got in the van. In the fun of shopping, she'd nearly forgotten the traveling part . . . and that it involved flying.

"Five days from now you'll be on your

way," Andrea told her as she started the engine.

"Five days." Simone swallowed hard.

"Did you look at that workbook last night?"

"I read the whole first section. I even practiced the deep breathing relaxation technique."

"And?"

"And then I fell asleep."

Andrea laughed. "Well, then it must work."

Simone sighed. "Hopefully." But as they drove back home, she wasn't so sure. She still remembered the photos of the small twisted and charred plane that Grandpa and his buddy Owen had gone down in. The pictures were so ghastly that she wouldn't even let Grandma see them. So horrible . . . so tragic . . . so unforgettable.

The next few days zipped by. And every time Simone considered canceling the trip, Andrea always seemed to be nearby, ready to talk her down, literally holding her hand at times, and even doing workbook exercises with her. Finally, she persuaded Simone this was the *right* thing to do. Simone owed it to Great-Grandmamma Simone Sophia — the woman who shared her name — to see this thing through.

So it was with that thought in mind that Simone found herself at a boarding gate in LAX, waiting for a flight to Seattle. Dressed in a chic pair of jeans and stylish boots topped with a cool embroidered coat-style cardigan and knotted scarf, Simone just wished she felt as confident as she looked. The dog-eared workbook tucked into her tapestry carry-on bag had a section called "Fake It till You Make It." That was what she was trying to do today. Act like she was an experienced flyer with no anxiety, fear, or white-knuckled panic.

But when it was time to board the plane, her chest pounded so hard that she worried it could be a heart attack. She'd read about that in the workbook. *"A panic attack can imitate a heart attack."* So she knew she shouldn't be surprised, shouldn't take it seriously. Just breathe and try to act composed. Fake it till you make it. When the flight attendant smiled and greeted her, Simone imitated the woman, greeting her back.

"Have a good flight," the attendant called out as Simone passed.

I am safe, I am fine, Simone repeated silently to herself as she made her way to her seat near the back of the plane, which, according to Andrea, was the safest place to sit in the unlikely event of a plane wreck.

Don't think about plane wrecks, she reminded herself. *I am safe, I am fine.* She shoved her tapestry bag into the hold above her row then slid past the seats, right next to the window where she fastened and tightened her seat belt. It had been Andrea's idea to have a window seat. "Less claustrophobic," she'd promised. But suddenly the idea of looking out and seeing the world so far below felt terrifying. *Keep your eyes closed,* she told herself. *And pray. Pray, pray, pray.*

So that is what she did. She could hear people moving about, stowing luggage, getting into their seats, but she kept her eyes tightly closed — breathing deeply. Hopefully other passengers would assume she was asleep. If only!

After what felt like hours, announcements were made, and the plane began to move. Still, Simone kept her eyes closed — and continued to pray. Only now she was praying that she wasn't about to have a real heart attack and need to be hauled out on a stretcher. Although being removed, even laid out on a gurney, suddenly felt preferable to dying in a plane crash. *Please, God, help me!*

CHAPTER 4

The flight to Seattle had to be the longest two and a half hours of Simone's entire life. It felt more like two and a half weeks! Despite closing her eyes after a frightening glance down during takeoff that nearly paralyzed her, and despite deep breathing, sincerely praying, and silently chanting mantras, she was emotionally exhausted by the time she stumbled down the ramp away from the plane. It was all she could do not to fall on her knees and kiss the floor of SeaTac air terminal once she got inside. But now what?

As humiliating as it would be to call Andrea and confess this was way too much for her, Simone wanted to pull the plug. Faking it wasn't making it. She was done with the charade. A bus ride back to LA wasn't ideal, but it was far better than this.

Looking for a quiet place to sit and make the awkward phone call to Andrea, Simone marveled at how calm and even happy the other travelers appeared. Apparently, none of them were the least bit concerned about bursting into flames and plummeting from the sky. She found a deserted gate, sat down, and pulled out her phone. Without even allowing Andrea to ask how she was doing, Simone poured out her story.

"I can't do this. I'm coming home," she finally sobbed. "It's too hard."

"Take a slow deep breath," Andrea said calmly. "Listen to me. You can do this, Simone. It wasn't easy, but you made it safely to Seattle, and you'll make it safely to Paris. And when you get to Paris and then on to Avre, you're going to thank me for this."

"I am not —"

"Shh! Listen to me. Look at your carry-on bag, okay? See the pocket on the side of it? Open that up and you'll see a little ziplock with —"

"What are you saying? Did you stash drugs in my bag?" Simone felt her anxiety rise again.

"No, not drugs, silly. It's just chocolate laced with some perfectly safe natural herbs that will help you relax. I was going to tell you about it before your Seattle flight, but the girls distracted me."

Simone opened the pocket to see several squares of harmless-looking chocolate. "Okay, I found the stash, but I don't think that's going to do it for me."

"It will work. I promise you. I used it a few times after the girls were born when I was having some postpartum anxiety."

"You had postpartum anxiety?" Simone felt bad. "I never knew that."

"Yeah, well, you were up in Sacramento then. And it wasn't like I told everyone about it. But those little chocolates really helped to calm me down. They're perfectly safe. The only side effect is they might make you sleepy. But if you're really suffering anxiety, they will probably just calm you down."

"Really?" Simone studied an innocent-looking dark chocolate square. "So, I just eat it?"

"Yes. Go ahead and eat one now. Are you at your gate for the Paris flight yet?"

Simone sighed. "No . . . I, uh, I wasn't sure I could do that."

"You can. You know you want to go to France. Eat one chocolate right now, then get yourself to your next gate. The herbs take about thirty minutes to kick in. After you're aboard the plane, if you still feel anxious, have another chocolate."

"I don't know about this." She sniffed the chocolate. "You're not just pulling my leg? Planting chocolate as a placebo?"

"No, of course not. Eat it and get to the next gate."

Simone popped a square into her mouth. "Tastes like chocolate."

"It *is* chocolate — and more. Now you need to head for your gate." Andrea spoke in the same tone she used while getting her girls ready for bed. "Take your time. Get settled in. Maybe find yourself something good to eat. And get some water or juice — no coffee — then just sit down and relax. And, oh yeah, don't forget to use the restroom. Then just read your workbook, breathe deeply, and call me if you need to. But you can do this, Simone. I know you can."

Simone wasn't so sure, but hearing Andrea's calm voice helped. Or maybe the chocolate was already kicking in. But as she stood, she assured Andrea she'd give it her best shot. Another calming breath and she set out to find the next gate. Maybe she could do this after all. And if not, she would just cut her losses and go home.

It seemed slightly miraculous, not to mention surreal, when Simone found herself

46

seated on her next flight. It was a larger, more comfortable plane, and it even smelled good. The music was pleasing and the flight attendants polite. All in all, everything seemed much, much better. Or maybe it was her. Or more likely the chocolate. Thanks to Andrea's counsel, assuring her it couldn't hurt, Simone had now consumed three squares, and her anxiety level, though still nibbling at her heels, seemed to have shrunk considerably. According to Andrea she would be dozing off soon. Hopefully before takeoff.

"Hello." A dark-haired man in a brown tweed jacket smiled down at Simone. "This seat taken?"

She blinked. "Aren't the seats assigned?"

"Sorry. My pathetic attempt at humor." He chuckled as he shoved a leather bag overhead. "That's my seat next to you."

"Oh, right . . . I'm not a very seasoned flyer." She forced an embarrassed smile as he slid into the middle seat, but felt relieved she'd made her last restroom stop, taking time to put on some deodorant, brush her teeth, and freshen up some.

"I haven't flown anywhere myself lately. Not for at least five years." He fumbled to buckle his seat belt. "But at least this plane's roomier than I remember. That's because it's an international flight."

"Well, it feels better than my flight here — *that* was a nightmare." She tried not to obsess over the term *international flight.* Was she really about to fly over an ocean?

"A nightmare?" His dark brows arched. "What happened?"

"Oh, nothing really." Feeling silly, she looked down, twisting one of the big wooden buttons on her cardigan. "To be honest, that was my first time on a plane."

"Oh." He nodded. "I see."

"And, well, I have this fear of flying. I was a little freaked."

"You seem pretty calm now."

"That's because my friend gave me anti-anxiety chocolates."

"Seriously?"

She eagerly nodded. "They're pretty good. Want one?"

He laughed. "No, I don't think I need one. I'm okay." He tucked his iPad into the pocket in front of him then turned to look at her.

"Oh, good. I didn't know. I mean, I assume everyone else is flying fearlessly. At least it looks like they are." She smiled nervously. She wasn't usually this chatty with strangers. Maybe it was the chocolate. "I just hope I don't make you uncomfortable . . . I mean if I should suddenly have a full-blown panic attack right over the middle of the Atlantic Ocean — don't be too alarmed."

His brows shot up. "Do you really think you will?"

"I honestly don't know, but just mentioning the phrase *panic attack* is pretty disturbing."

"Then don't mention it." His hazel eyes twinkled. "And I'm no expert, but for your first day of flying, you seem to be off to a pretty good start."

"How's that?"

"Well, for starters, you seem relatively calm right now. And you're well put together." He pointed to the book and magazine tucked in the chair pocket in front of Simone, her water bottle, sanitizing wipes, neck pillow, earbuds. "You could easily pass for a very experienced world traveler."

"I had coaching."

He smiled. "Besides that, here you are — on your way to Paris. And in wintertime. Not everyone does that. I assume you're traveling on your own." He glanced around.

She nodded. "That's true. I am."

"Well, that's very impressive. And adventuresome too."

"I guess it might look that way, but the

truth is my best friend pressured me to do this. I think she'd disown me if I bailed."

"Why's that?" His eyes seemed full of compassion.

It was as if someone had uncorked her bottle — the whole story of selling Grandma's house and Andrea's assistance poured out. "I honestly planned to pull the plug at the last minute," she finally confessed, "but here I am . . . on my way."

"Embarking on what I'm sure will be an unforgettable adventure."

"Unforgettable as in I'll live to remember it?" she said in a teasing tone, although she was partially serious. "Maybe share the story with my grandchildren someday."

"Yes, of course. I'll tell you what helps me most when I'm anxious or afraid." He looked deeply into her eyes. "It's prayer. I find that when I hand these troubles over to God, I start to relax. I trust him for the outcome, and I've never been let down."

She sighed. "I've honestly been trying to do that." She thought of how many other things she'd prayed about in her lifetime — things that had been beyond her control, but her prayers never seemed to get answered quite the way she'd hoped. "But sometimes it's hard to pray."

"Maybe it's the hardness of praying that

50

makes it better." He paused as the plane's engine grew louder.

She wanted to ask him what he meant, but the flight attendant started going over the emergency procedures. Noticing how her seatmate paid close attention, Simone did likewise, but she was stuck on what he'd just said about prayer — did harder really make it better? How was that?

Watching the young woman demonstrate the use of the oxygen mask, flotation device, and emergency exits, Simone grew more and more unnerved. By the time the attendant finished, Simone's heart was racing again. Her chest grew tighter, and it was hard to breathe. Was there enough air in here? She suddenly wanted to leap over the nice fellow beside her, climb past the older man next to him, and push her way to the front where she would demand to be let off. She could claim a heart attack, which probably wasn't far from the truth.

"You okay?" her seatmate asked quietly.

"I, uh, I don't know." She could feel her hands shaking uncontrollably.

"You look a little pale," he whispered. "Panic attack?"

She barely nodded, gripping the armrests so tightly she thought they might break off. Every muscle in her body was clenched and tight, and it took every ounce of control not to scream, "Let me off!"

"Just breathe," he said softly. "Close your eyes . . . imagine how beautiful Paris is going to be." As the plane began to back up, he continued to speak in the same soothing tone, telling her how stunning the city looked in December. Almost as if he were reading from a travel brochure or telling her a story. "It gets darker earlier this time of year so that will make the lights on the Champs-Élysées seem even brighter, there will be less crowds, shops won't be so busy, and the air will be clearer."

"Have you been to Paris before?" She cautiously opened her eyes, peering curiously at him as the plane taxied toward the runway.

"I was there one summer, during college. It was hot and crowded and busy then. But still beautiful. Well worth seeing. My good friend Sasha had lived there for a few years. She showed me all around, but I remember her saying it was wonderful in December. She said winter was the perfect time to visit."

"Interesting." Simone nodded. "I never considered that."

"Sasha moved back to Seattle a few years ago. She and I got together just last week, and she told me to be sure to visit the Christmas market. I guess it's pretty cool. She went on and on about Parisian Christmas decorations. Not cheesy like what you see in America but artistic and beautiful. And, of course, there's always the food." He sighed as the plane began to pick up speed. "Don't get me going on French cuisine." He actually smacked his lips, which made Simone smile.

The plane was too noisy to hear much of anything as it took off, but Simone simply closed her eyes, allowing images of Paris decorated for Christmas and thoughts of delicious Parisian food to occupy her thoughts. As the jet soared upward, her anxiety seemed to be left down below. When she finally opened her eyes, she felt surprisingly calm. Was it the chocolate or the handsome guy seated next to her? Whatever it was, she had no complaints.

"You seem better," he said as she sat up straighter.

"I feel better." She smiled. "Thanks for your help. It was fun hearing more about Paris in December. I have a booklet about Paris in my bag, but I haven't read much yet."

"No problem. Sasha wanted to be sure I didn't miss a thing. I think she was wishing she could come too."

"Oh." Simone nodded. "Is she your girl-friend?" Of course, she instantly regretted this — it was none of her business who Sasha was.

"Sasha's just a good friend." He grinned. "By the way, I'm Kyle. I guess I should've said that before."

She felt relieved. "I'm Simone."

"Simone? That sounds French."

"It is French. *Simone Sophia.* After my great-grandmother. She was French."

"Cool. I assume you're going to search out your heritage?"

"I guess. You see, my great-grandfather was in Europe during World War II. He was an Army Air Corps navigator. But his plane got shot down over France. That's how he met my great-grandmother."

"Romantic. So is that why you're afraid of flying? Because of your great-grandfather being shot down."

"It probably didn't help. Although when I grew up hearing that story, it always sounded more like a fun adventure. Fortunately, he had a parachute. And of course, that's how he found his true love. So happy ending." She frowned. "Not so much for his son though. My grandpa was killed in a small plane accident about fifteen years ago.

That's when I developed my flying phobia."

"I'm sorry. What a tragic way to lose a grandfather."

"Yeah, and he was more like a father. My grandparents raised me. Anyway, they're both gone now."

"Again, I'm sorry." His expression looked genuinely sad for her. Then he brightened. "But let's not forget, you're on your way to Paris. Paris in December. What could be better than that?"

"I guess it could be better if we were already there." She sneaked a glance out the window then shuddered. Even though the plane was encompassed by clouds, it was unsettling. She was suddenly aware that they were high in the air with nothing to hold them up but those engines. What if one blew up? The only way out was down. She turned back around, grabbing the armrests like a lifeline.

"Feeling shaky again?" he asked.

"Uh-huh . . . unfortunately." She stared straight ahead, trying to erase the thoughts of engines exploding.

"Just lean back and breathe," he said quietly. "Think happy thoughts."

"I'll try," she muttered. "Sorry to be such a downer. Feel free to ignore me."

He laughed. "No worries."

She closed her eyes, taking in a long deep breath and slowly exhaling. "If you're lucky, I'll go to sleep and stop bothering you."

"You're no bother, Simone. Just think about Paris in December . . . how beautiful it will be," he reminded her. So that's exactly what she did. And it was mostly working, but she was craving another chocolate. They were in her bag stowed above them, and she didn't want to make everyone move to get it. *I am safe, I am fine,* she told herself, but her hands still grasped the armrests.

While taking another long deep breath and doing the counting that was supposed to help, she could hear Kyle engaged with someone else. Part of her felt sorry because she had enjoyed his company, but another part of her felt relieved. He deserved a better seatmate than Ms. Flight-o-phobia.

He nudged her arm. "Here, Simone, try this."

She opened her eyes to see him holding a small glass of red wine. "What?" She sat up straighter, blinking.

"It's complimentary pinot noir from France. It might help you to relax." As he handed it to her, the attendant handed Kyle another one. "Here's to Paris." Kyle held up his glass like a toast.

"To Paris." She sighed. "May we get there ASAP."

He chuckled and they both took a sip. "Not bad for complimentary wine," he said. "And under the circumstances, it's a smart move on the airline's part. I'm sure a lot of people feel nervous about flying. They just know how to hide it better."

"So everyone's just pretending?" She told him about the fake it until you make it exercise. "I thought it was working earlier today, before I started to unravel."

"Well, if it's any comfort, I think you're doing just fine. By the time you fly back home, you'll be an old pro."

"Flying back home." She frowned. "Not sure I care to think about that now."

He laughed. "I get you. So, tell me, how long will you be in Paris?"

"Only a few days. But I'll be in France until after New Year's."

"That's great. And you'll be looking up your great-grandmother's family?"

"That's my plan, but I'm not sure they're even still around. My great-grandmamma didn't really stay in touch with them. In fact, I sometimes got the feeling she left under unhappy circumstances."

"Maybe her family resented her marrying

an American. Some French don't care for us."

"I don't know. But I'm curious to find out more." She told him a bit about the mysterious letter and treasure. "I seriously doubt that any such treasure still exists, but I feel like I'm doing this for my namesake."

"Interesting . . . and fun too."

Weary of talking about herself, she smiled at him. "So what takes you to Paris? Well, besides this plane?"

"You must be feeling better — you have a sense of humor." He grinned. "I'm not going only to Paris. Although I do plan to spend some time there and see how it looks at Christmastime. I also have other places to see and go to as well. It's kind of a long story."

She leaned back, watching him with interest. "We've got lots of time."

He chuckled. "That's true. Where do I begin?"

"At the beginning?"

He told her about growing up in Seattle and about this older neighbor named Claude Aron who had come to the States from France. "Claude was sort of like a grandpa to me. He actually taught me my first French words and helped me to become somewhat fluent. He's the one who told me I needed to go to Paris as a young man. The reason I took that trip back in college."

"I had dreamed of traveling to Europe after high school," Simone said, "but then my grandpa died . . . plans had to change."

As the plane traveled steadily, they continued to learn more about each other. Kyle told her about how his dad had passed away too. "It was just last summer. That's part of why I'm taking this trip. My dad's parents immigrated from Norway before he was born. During the Great Depression. My dad always dreamed of going to Norway after he retired, but then he got cancer . . . and never got the chance."

"Now it's my turn to say I'm sorry for your loss."

"Yeah. It all seemed to happen so fast. Anyway, my mom decided that since I was planning to go to France anyway, I should just bring Dad's ashes with me. She thought they should be scattered in a fjord near his ancestors' hometown. Sort of like he finally made it." Kyle looked sad.

She considered this. "I'll bet your dad would be happy to think that you'll get to see Norway."

"Yeah." He brightened. "And I always wanted to see Norway. Although I'd have rather gone with Dad. Anyway, I'll spend a few days there . . . and then I'll head down to France and Switzerland."

"And what will you do in France and Switzerland?"

"Well, would you believe that I'm a clock-maker?" He grinned.

"Seriously? Is that a real career? It sounds like something from a previous century."

"It's real — but rare." His mouth twisted to one side. "To be accurate, I'm really more of an apprentice clockmaker. And that might be a stretch to claim that."

"A person can really make a living at clockmaking?"

"It depends on how you define 'a living.' I suppose if you're a really excellent clock-maker and you don't live too extravagantly." He rubbed his chin. "Fortunately, I'm not too concerned about finances. A friend and I started a software games company back in college. No complaints . . . it's done okay. But even while designing games and soft-ware, I still loved to work on clocks in my spare time. Either building new ones or fix-ing old ones. I used to joke that clocks helped me *unwind.*"

She chuckled. "I sort of get that."

"Anyway, after all that time in the tech world, I was ripe for change. I guess my dad's death last summer sort of prompted the whole thing. It hit me hard to see his life end before he got to attack his bucket list. So I sold off my half of the company —"

"To become a clockmaker?" She smiled with interest.

"Yep. But it didn't take long to figure out there's a whole lot I don't know about clockmaking."

"So how does one learn about clockmaking? Is there a special school? How did you learn about it in the first place?"

"Remember my elderly neighbor — Claude Aron? Well, he's the one who got me interested in clocks. He'd been a clockmaker in France. Actually, he worked at a watch factory but made clocks on the side. He was Jewish, and when Hitler rose into power, he and his family fled to America. Anyway, Claude was about eighty when he and I became friends, and he taught me everything I know about clocks and watches." Kyle held out his right arm, pushing up his sleeve to reveal a classically styled watch. "He gave this to me for my eighth-grade graduation. Not long before he passed away."

She peered down at the watch. "Is it a Rolex?"

He slowly nodded. "Yeah. Made in Geneva, Switzerland. Not too far from where Claude's family came from. He got it in the 1930s."

"It must be valuable."

"Valuable to me. And, yeah, it's worth a lot to collectors too. Not that I'm parting with it." He smoothed his thumb over the watch face. "It's my treasure."

She nodded, suddenly remembering her treasure and how it was the motivation for this trip. But really, she felt fairly certain this was a wild-goose chase. A wild-goose chase that was transporting her across the Atlantic Ocean . . . and strangely enough she no longer felt terribly concerned. Mostly she felt sleepy.

When Simone woke up, it was dark outside. Perhaps that was good. She lowered the window shade and silently repeated her mantra. *I am safe, I am fine.*

"Hey, Sleeping Beauty is awake," Kyle said.

She couldn't help but smile. "That was a nice nap. What time is it?"

"Paris time?"

She shrugged. "I guess."

"I already reset my watch." He checked his Rolex. "It's 4:47 a.m. in Paris."

"And we're supposed to arrive a little before one." She tried to compute the numbers, frowning to think she still had seven hours of flying time. "I wonder what time it is in LA? I guess I should check my phone."

"I usually try to forget home time when traveling. Helps ward off jet lag." His brow creased as if doing the math. "But it would be 7:47 p.m. on the West Coast."

"Wow, that late. I must've been asleep for a while."

He nodded. "You did have a nice nap."

"Hopefully I didn't snore."

He chuckled. "No, but you chattered away in your sleep — revealed all kinds of deep dark secrets."

She sat up straight. "Seriously?"

"Kidding." He held up his hands. "Sorry."

She felt relieved. Especially since she'd just woken from a pleasant dream — about Kyle! A dream she'd be embarrassed to have him privy to. "So if it's nearly eight in LA, that would explain why I'm ravenous."

"They served dinner while you were sleeping, but I thought you might be hungry. I asked them to save yours." Kyle waved to the attendant, indicating that Simone was ready for her dinner.

She thanked him and was soon dining on

slightly dry chicken and vegetables and rice. Still, it was hot and better than nothing. As she ate, she asked Kyle more questions about his clockmaking plans. "I think we left off with you telling me about how Claude mentored you as a clockmaker, but is that why you're going to France? I can't quite remember."

"Yes. Claude sometimes spoke of the region he'd grown up in back in France. Not too far from the Rolex factory in Geneva. Apparently, there were a number of expert clockmakers in his region. So, I plan to explore, visit a few watch factories and clock companies, and I've even contacted some private clockmakers. Almost everyone's been very welcoming. And if I find the right spot, I might do a short apprenticeship. Acquire some new skills. Rather 'old' skills. I want to make clocks the way they did a hundred or more years ago."

She wiped her mouth with the tiny napkin that came with her meal. "How interesting. And after your apprenticeship ends? Will you remain in France?"

"I'm not sure. But my dream is to have my own clock and watch shop someday."

"What a wonderful dream."

After she finished her meal, Kyle pulled

out his iPad. "How's your French?" he asked.

She considered this. "Well, I haven't really practiced much since high school, but I did bring a little handbook that I've been studying these last few days."

"Good for you. I downloaded an English-to-French program. Want to brush up?"

"Sure." She nodded. "What a great way to pass the time."

Together they practiced some dialogues and did vocabulary tests and even played a couple of games. But after an hour or so, Simone felt the plane shifting, almost as if they were descending. "What's happening?" She grabbed his arm. "It feels like we're going down."

He put his iPad back into the chair pocket. "You're right. We *are* going down."

"But it's too soon. Paris must still be several hours away. We must be over the Atlantic right now." She searched his face for answers, surprised that he seemed this calm despite their clear descent. "What's going on, Kyle? What's wrong? Why are we going down in the middle of the ocean?"

Before he could answer, the flight attendants announced that passengers should return to their seats, fasten their seat belts, and put their tray tables up to prepare for landing. The pilot said something too, but Simone's mind spun so wildly that she couldn't make it out. She didn't need anyone to tell her what lay ahead. It was just as she'd predicted — they were about to plummet into the icy Atlantic Ocean. She closed her eyes and desperately prayed.

CHAPTER 5

"Iceland?" Simone repeated what Kyle had just told her following a somewhat bumpy landing, which to her relief was not in the ocean. "Why are we in Iceland?" She lowered her voice. "Have we been hijacked?"

"No." Kyle chuckled. "You didn't know this flight connects in Iceland?"

"I had no idea." She peered out the window only to see darkness and blue runway lights passing by as the plane taxied toward the terminal. She turned back to Kyle. "I still don't get it. I mean, Iceland? It seems a bit off the beaten path from Paris."

"Well, it's a shorter route to fly over the Artic Circle. And since you booked your flight on Icelandair —"

"I didn't book this flight, my friend did." She sighed. "I refused to take a nonstop flight from LA to Paris. . . . I was afraid to be in a plane for so long."

"Well, Reykjavik is Icelandair's hub, which

is why they connect here," he said. "That's why the flight was so cheap."

"And Paris?" she asked, feeling dumb.

"After this, it's straight to Paris." As the plane stopped, Kyle unbuckled his seat belt and, already, other passengers were standing up and gathering their things.

"Are we supposed to get off the plane?" She felt fully discombobulated now.

"I am. And you should too. There's a ninety-minute layover. Nice chance to stretch your legs. Just grab your carry-on. Later you'll reboard since this plane continues to Paris." He stood, looking down the aisle to where other passengers were lined up to exit.

Still confused and curious about the time, Simone reached for her bag, extracted her phone, then waited for it to power up. When it did, she was surprised to see it was nearly midnight in LA. No wonder she felt so fuzzy, she should be sleeping soundly right now. She looked up to see Kyle about to exit the plane. He waved and smiled. Not willing to miss out on more time with him, Simone grabbed her things and hurried to get off the plane.

"What time is it here?" she asked Kyle as she caught up with him.

"About eight a.m.," he said. "Want to get

some coffee? Or some breakfast?"

"Breakfast?" She considered how it was midnight back home then agreed. Not because she was hungry, but because she wanted to be with Kyle.

When they were finally seated at a table with their coffees, Simone began to relax. "It's good to be on solid ground again." She sipped her latte and sighed.

"I have to commend you on how well you did on that flight." He lifted his coffee to toast her. "Well done."

"You mean in between panic attacks?"

He smiled. "At least the attacks didn't last too long."

"I really thought we were crash-landing into the ocean," she confessed sheepishly. "I was preparing to die."

"And here we are alive and well and about to have an Icelandic breakfast."

Kyle's order involved a large plate of meats and cheeses while Simone's was merely yogurt and granola. But it was being with Kyle that made it special. Already Simone was imagining spending time with him in Paris. Oh, he hadn't said anything specifically about this, but based on how he was treating her . . . well, it just seemed likely. They were just finishing when Kyle checked his watch.

"Uh-oh." He wiped his mouth with a napkin. "I'm going to have to make a run for it."

"A run for it?" She frowned up at the clock in the café. "Our flight's not supposed to leave for —"

"*My* flight leaves in fifteen minutes." He laid some tip money on the table and stood.

"Your flight?"

"To Oslo." He grabbed his bag, throwing a strap over his shoulder. "They've probably boarded. Sorry to dash out like this."

"Oslo?" She stood. "I thought you were going to Paris."

"*After* Oslo." He pulled out his phone. "Hurry, Simone. Walk with me to the gate. It's right over there. Give me your phone number so we can reconnect in Paris."

She picked up her bag and followed him, calling out the digits as they jogged to the gate that was nearly empty. Then, after a quick goodbye and a surprising kiss from Kyle (on the cheek!), he was gone. For some inexplicable reason Simone felt more alone than ever. As she walked back to the gate for the Paris flight, she felt a lump growing in her throat.

After reboarding her plane and returning to the same seat, tears began to trickle down. She knew it was silly. Good grief, she'd only known Kyle for a few hours . . . and yet it seemed like a year. Besides, hadn't he promised to get together with her in Paris? And what about that kiss? Did it mean something? Or was he just very demonstrative?

It was odd sitting there in the nearly empty plane. Only a few people had remained aboard: a mom with an infant, an elderly couple, a pair of teens stretched out across the empty seats and sleeping. The general atmosphere was quiet and peaceful. And to her relief, she no longer felt anxious and nervous. Just sad. Very sad. And lonely.

The plane slowly began to reload with noisy passengers and eventually taxied out for takeoff. This time she didn't freak out. She didn't have a death grip on the armrests. But as she looked at the empty seat beside her, she missed her seatmate. More than she cared to admit. She desperately hoped that in her rush to spew out her phone number, he'd gotten it right — and she wanted to kick herself for not getting his number. She didn't even know his last name. Just Kyle. Kyle from Seattle. Kyle the clockmaker from Seattle . . . on his way to Oslo. She tried to recall how long he planned to stay in Norway. Probably longer than she planned to stay in Paris. Had she even mentioned she'd only be there a few days?

Despite her gloom about not having Kyle's pleasant companionship in Paris, Simone instantly fell in love with the beautiful city. Gaping out the window, as the taxi transported her from Charles de Gaulle Airport to her hotel in the city, she felt like a starry-eyed tourist but didn't even care. There was so much to see! She'd already left a message with Andrea, assuring her that she'd safely arrived, and downplaying her bouts with flying phobia. She thanked her friend for pushing her to take this trip, promising to tell her more about it later.

Although she'd planned to take a nap, once she entered the elegant old hotel and used her stilted French in order to check her bags until her room was available, she suddenly lost all desire to sleep. Her previous exhaustion from the long flight seemed to have evaporated in the damp Parisian air. So, dressed in a long warm coat and comfortable boots, she spent Friday afternoon strolling the charming streets and seeing the picturesque sights, finally stopping for an early dinner at a small café not far from her hotel.

As she sat by the window in the café, it

was already getting dark outside, and golden lights began to twinkle and glimmer up and down the avenue. With the pavement still damp from the afternoon rain, the scene reminded her of a French impressionist painting. Jaw-droppingly gorgeous. She glanced around the busy café, curious as to why other diners weren't staring out the window like she was. Because it looked truly magical. It was all she could do to control herself from yelling out to the rest of them, "Look, look — you're missing it!"

It felt a bit strange to eat alone in the most romantic city in the world. Once again, she found herself missing Kyle. More than ever. Sure, it seemed a little crazy since — she reminded herself again — she'd only known him a few hours. Hopefully he was enjoying Norway. And hopefully he had her phone number.

As she went to bed, she wondered if she'd overblown her time with him. Had her phobia of flying made his empathy and help seem more than it was? Had she imagined his interest in her was something beyond that of a concerned fellow traveler? But he'd asked for her number? Still, she knew it was best to let it go and simply enjoy her time here in Paris. *Que sera, sera . . . whatever will be, will be.*

73

Simone spent all day Saturday visiting even more sights. Playing the tourist, she'd booked a bus tour that promised the "full Parisian experience." She knew she had a lot to soak in and just three short days to do it. But all the while, getting on and off the bus at the various highlights, including the Eiffel Tower, Notre-Dame (which, thanks to reconstruction, had to be viewed from the street), the Louvre Museum, and more, she'd kept her phone handy and turned on, just in case Kyle should call.

She wondered if perhaps he'd already scattered his father's ashes . . . maybe he was on his way to Paris by now. Although that seemed a bit too fast. Still, it would've been fun to experience these remarkable places with him. Not on a bus like this . . . but for an inexperienced traveler alone, it seemed a wise choice. And, really, the tour was enjoyable, and the tour guide was interesting. Yet by the end of the day, she felt discouraged and a bit disappointed. Still no word from Kyle.

She was just getting off the bus when the tour guide announced their company still had a few seats available for the City of

Lights night tour. "We embark at seven. Two hours of Christmas lights and champagne," he told her. "Trust me — this sight — you do not want to miss." And so, Simone bought a ticket, and after a quick bite to eat, climbed back onto the tour bus.

As they rambled through the festively lit city, leisurely moving past many of the sights she'd already seen by daylight, like the Eiffel Tower, Champs-Élysées, and Arc de Triomphe, Simone felt completely awestruck. The city by night was luminous magic . . . like another world. Glittering Christmas trees lined avenues, strings of lights reflected over the river, and Viaduc des Arts and Place Vendôme sparkled like glittering treasure chests. The entire city was illuminated for the holidays. Even better than what Kyle had described on the plane. Although it made her a bit blue to remember her seatmate. If only he were here!

As she returned to her hotel, she felt silly for caring so much about a man she barely knew. Kyle obviously had not felt the same way. He was simply a nice guy trying to lend a helping hand, and it was ridiculous for her to continue obsessing over him. As she went up to her room, she recalled what he'd said about how difficult prayers . . . that they were the best prayers . . . or something to that effect. So she prayed that his time in Norway would be wonderful and all he hoped for, and she prayed that when he eventually made it to Paris, he would enjoy it as much as she had.

Even though Sunday was her last full day in Paris, Simone no longer felt driven to take in everything. By now she realized that could take months, possibly years. Plus, she was a little worn out from the time change and all her sightseeing. Today was a day to slowly soak in the quieter beauty of the city, which seemed to be resting as well. After a midday stroll, between rain showers and stopping by Sainte-Chapelle Cathedral for a quiet moment of prayer, she was content to return to her hotel for an afternoon cup of tea and a plate of delectable pastries.

Then, grateful for her charmingly old-world room, she packed her bags in preparation for tomorrow's train ride. Simone had no idea what she would find in Avre, or if any relatives still lived there, but she wanted to arrive with all her bearings and not overly bedraggled. She went downstairs for another early dinner.

Once again, it felt a bit lonely to dine alone in the City of Love, but at least the restaurant wasn't too busy at this hour, and the food, as usual, was delicious. Afterward, she wandered outside to admire the luminous splendor of Paris by night one last time, taking a few photos on her phone to send to Andrea. Noticing she'd received no new calls, she went back inside, trying not to feel disappointed over Kyle's silence. Looking forward to a nice hot bath with the hotel's lovely toiletries, she knew it was best to forget about Kyle and be grateful he'd been there when she needed a friend.

Before she went to bed, she prayed once again that his path would go smoothly in Norway and later in France . . . and that God would bless his pursuit of an apprenticeship and subsequent career as a clockmaker. *Kyle the clockmaker.* For some reason the thought made her smile. *God bless Kyle the clockmaker!* From now on, Simone was determined to put the clockmaker out of her mind . . . and heart.

CHAPTER 6

Already Simone felt that her French was improving. The taxi driver seemed to understand her perfectly when she asked him to transport her to Gare du Nord — and soon she was in front of the Paris train station. Like everything else in Paris, Gare du Nord was beautiful. The front of the stone castle with its high-arched windows looked so elegant that she momentarily doubted it was truly a train station. But seeing other travelers going in and out with luggage, she decided this must be the right place.

The high, curved ceilings inside the terminal resembled a cathedral. After getting directions to the correct platform, she felt glad she'd come early. She leisurely strolled through the cavernous building and, since she'd skipped breakfast, she had plenty of time to get a latte and croissant to take with her. Strolling toward her platform with her smaller bag over a shoulder, her wheeled bag trailing behind her, and her coffee in hand, she imagined herself a seasoned traveler. And knowing this leg of her journey would never leave the ground actually made her smile.

Even so, it felt exciting to board the sleek silver train. It felt jarringly modern compared to the old-world Parisian culture she'd just enjoyed, and the interior was clean and comfortable. She took a seat by the window and made herself at home, setting out her coffee, pastry, and the novel she'd barely begun to read. So far so good. Wasn't this what real seasoned travelers might do?

Between gazing out the window and covertly observing passengers, many who appeared to be headed for ski slopes, Simone was not the least bit bored. Without a doubt, she preferred train travel to flying. Too bad no train could cross the Atlantic. It wasn't long before the Parisian buildings dissolved into less-populated, more suburban-looking areas. Eventually they were passing through the countryside with charming small towns along the way. Between the towns were numerous farms and fields, many with livestock like cattle, sheep, or goats. And, of course, there were vineyards. But because of recent rains, it all had a slightly soggy, quiet appearance . . . as if the land were resting for winter. Simone tried to imagine how green and alive it might appear in the springtime. Would she ever be back that time of year?

After a few hours, she realized it was nearly two and she was hungry. Seeing other passengers leaving and returning with food, she decided to do some exploring for herself. She picked up her bag and, acting like she knew where she was going, followed a young couple through a few cars only to discover they were headed to the rear of the train to smoke cigarettes. Embarrassed, she pretended to be stretching her legs as she turned around and proceeded in the other direction. Eventually she found the buffet car and got herself a light lunch and returned to her seat.

She was just finishing up when she realized the train was heading into hills dusted with snow. It didn't take long before the dusting turned into deeper snow, thick and fresh and white. They were obviously at the foot of the French Alps now. Feeling almost childlike, she leaned toward the window, peering out and watching the snowy whiteness in wide-eyed wonder. She was not in Southern California anymore!

Simone felt like a character in an old movie as she got off the train in Avre. She remembered watching *Dr. Zhivago* with Grandma as a teen, and besides being a very long movie, it had involved a lot of snow. And Avre had a lot of snow. Fortunately, she had on her boots and warm coat, but the cold wind still cut through her as she hurried into the bright red two-story train station. She was pleased to find it was warm inside.

It took a couple of attempts to speak in stilted French before Simone pulled out the little notebook where she'd penned her travel information (in case her phone battery died) and showed it to the woman behind the desk. The woman spoke quickly in French, pointing this way and that, suggesting that Simone could walk. Then finally, looking at Simone's luggage, she said what sounded like "take a taxi." So that's what Simone did.

Although the hotel really wasn't that far from the train station, Simone was glad she hadn't attempted to walk. She couldn't imagine dragging her wheeled bag through about a foot of freshly fallen snow. Although people were out with snow shovels, there were lots of spots that had yet to be cleared. Still, it was so beautiful — so white and pristine and, thanks to the sunshine, glistening — that she couldn't wait to get out and walk around in this winter wonderland. After she put on some more layers of clothing!

The hotel looked very much like the photo that Andrea had shown her last week. Was it really only a week ago? With its steep-angled roof and high narrow windows, it resembled a chalet. Covered with snow, it was charming and sweet. The interior wasn't disappointing either. The beautiful front desk was intricately carved with bears and rabbits, trees and leaves. And the big stone fireplace had a crackling fire. On the wood-plank floors were worn Persian rugs with several large pieces of furniture — from antiques to big leather chairs and sofas — here and there. All looked very inviting.

"Bonjour, mademoiselle!" a man called as he carried in a load of firewood, depositing it into a box by the fireplace. Then continuing to speak in rapid French, some she understood but most she didn't, he waved her over to the big reception desk. In broken French she explained her language challenges and told him her name. To her surprise, he replied in English.

"Ah, Miss Winthrop, welcome to Château Edelweiss."

"You speak English!" she exclaimed happily.

"Yes. I studied in London." He waved his hand. "To be a good innkeeper, I want to speak fluently."

"Oh, that's so nice. I've just come from Paris where, it seems, no one speaks English."

"Aha. Did you travel well?"

"Yes." She eagerly nodded. "It was a lovely train ride, and the snow made everything so pretty."

"You like snow?" His blue eyes twinkled with interest as he removed an index card from a file box.

"I haven't had much experience with it," she said, "but I do think it's beautiful."

"Then you are in the right place."

She smiled. "Good."

He stuck out his hand. "I am Noel Durand. Welcome to my family's inn."

"Thank you, Mr. Durand." She shook his hand.

"Please, call me Noel." He tipped his head politely.

"Okay. Thank you, Noel."

"And you? You are from California?" He looked at the index card.

"Yes."

"Traveling alone?" Noel turned around to pluck a brass key from a board with numerous hooks.

"Uh . . . yes." She wondered about this inquisitiveness but figured he must already know these answers anyway.

He turned back around. "And coming to Avre . . . in wintertime? So close to Christmas . . . are you a ski enthusiast?"

"No." She shook her head.

"You have family here?" He tilted his head to one side.

"Maybe." She grimaced, unsure of how much to reveal. Really, was this any of his business?

"Aha. You are looking for long-lost relations then."

"Sort of." She pursed her lips. Sure, Noel seemed a nice enough fellow, and he was certainly handsome with his blonde curls and blue eyes, but she didn't appreciate his prying.

He glanced back down at the index card. "But this name, *Winthrop,* it is not French."

"No." She studied him, wondering if perhaps he might actually be helpful to her mission. "My family name — I mean my great-grandmamma's — is *Beaumont.*"

"Ah — Beaumont. That is common name

in Avre."

"Common?" She frowned.

"Oh, not so common as Bernard or Martin." He pointed to himself. "Or even Durand. But, yes, there is Beaumonts in Avre." He handed her the brass key.

"A real key." She fingered the cool metal. "Not a card."

"My maman — she insists on old ways." He waved the index card before slipping it back into the wooden box then pointed to a nearby computer screen. "But this — this is for me. Best of both worlds."

Simone smiled. "I see."

"Now I will show you to your room." He rounded the desk and picked up her bags. "This way." He started to head for the big carved staircase, but then he paused. "You are on top floor, Miss Winthrop. You are good with stairs, no?"

"Yes. Stairs are fine."

"Good. No lift." He shrugged. "Some older hotels install lifts, but Maman, she say no." He chuckled. "The stairs are good for the legs."

"And they are beautiful." She ran her hand over the carved banister. "Is this an old building?"

"Circa 1910. My great-grandparents build it."

"And the name? Château Edelweiss? Isn't edelweiss Austrian?"

"There is American misconception that edelweiss belongs to Austria," he said, "but origination is in Switzerland. You know we are closer to Geneva than Paris?"

"I noticed that on the map."

"My great-grandmamma, she was from Geneva. She named the château."

"How interesting."

"I have a friend," he said as he started up the next flight. "His name is Leon. Leon *Beaumont.* He owns Café Bleu. Maybe he is your relation?"

"I don't know. Maybe." She made a mental note of Café Bleu. "Does the Café Bleu serve dinner?"

"Oui." Noel paused at the top of the stairs. "I am happy to take you to meet my friend, Miss Winthrop. He does not speak English. I can interpret for you."

She wasn't sure about this. It was a generous offer, but was it wise to involve this somewhat snoopy innkeeper in her personal business? And yet . . . what difference would it make? She was an American looking for relatives in a small town at Christmastime — what was the point in trying to conceal something like that?

Noel set her bags by a carved wooden

door. "I hope you do not think I intrude." He looked genuinely apologetic. "Mamma, she say I am too enthusiastic sometimes."

Simone couldn't help but smile. "Enthusiasm is good sometimes. And, really, I would appreciate some help. I'd love for you to introduce me to your friend Leon Beaumont."

He brightened. "Très bien!"

"What time works for you?"

He checked his watch. "First, I call Leon, Miss Winthrop, to make reservation."

"Thank you, but please, call me Simone." She smiled gratefully.

"Oui. Simone. You meet me in lobby at six thirty then?"

Simone felt confused as she slid her key in the door. Had Noel actually invited her to dine with him at six thirty? Or to go and meet with Leon? Although if Leon ran a restaurant, wouldn't he be busy? Or was she just overthinking all of this? "Oui," she said as she opened the door. "Merci beaucoup."

Noel politely tipped his head. "De rien."

As she took her luggage into the room, she knew that *de rien* translated to "it's nothing." But was it nothing? Had she just agreed to a date with the innkeeper? And, really, what was wrong with that? He spoke excellent English and had a friend who might be her long-lost relative. Perhaps a fifth cousin thrice removed. Who knew? Why not just go with the flow and enjoy the evening? Wasn't that why she'd taken this trip? Or mostly anyway.

As she unpacked her bags, stowing clothes in an antique dresser and armoire, she remembered her *real* mission. Great-grandmamma Simone's treasure. That was why she was here. But it wasn't as if she could just announce this ridiculous notion to everyone she met. For one thing, they would probably assume she was crazy. Or even worse, they might become suspicious of an outsider trying to sneak in here and steal some family fortune. As if there were such a thing.

She removed the mysterious letter from her bag and read it again. And, although the very same letter had seemed rather bizarre and unbelievable back in California, it suddenly seemed a bit more real here in Avre. Especially in this charmingly rustic room with its rough beams and sloped ceiling. It seemed just the sort of room her great-grandmamma might've once occupied.

Simone pushed aside the lace curtains to gaze out the leaded glass window and couldn't help but gasp at the magical twilight outside. The dusky indigo sky had painted the snow-covered rooftops in shades of pale blue, and windows glowed amber as lights inside were turned on. Once again, Simone got the feeling she was someone else . . . somewhere else . . . or perhaps even traveling back in time. But it wasn't frightening. In fact, it was pretty exciting!

CHAPTER 7

Café Bleu was tucked into an old brick building that appeared to have apartments above. But as Simone got out of Noel's car, she noticed a sign on the door. "The café is closed," she said with concern.

"Oui. Is always closed on Monday, but Leon — he let us in." Noel knocked loudly on the glass door.

"He knows we're coming?" she asked.

"Oui, oui. He and Nicole — they expect us."

"Nicole?"

"Leon's wife and partner," he said.

An attractive young woman appeared behind the glass. After peering outside, she unlocked and opened the door. With a bright smile, she cheerfully greeted Noel.

"Entrez, s'il vous plaît." She waved them inside then closed and relocked the door. Suddenly she and Noel were speaking in rapid French, and then another man emerged from the kitchen, presumably Leon, and all three chattered so fast that Simone felt lost. But as introductions were made, Noel switched to English.

"I told them who you are, where you come from, and why you are here," he told her as Leon helped remove their coats. "Leon is eager to know who your relative is and if you are related to him."

Leon led them to a table set with four places and pulled out a chair. "Venez vous asseoir ici, s'il vous plait, Simone."

She thanked him as she sat, watching as Nicole, still chattering with Noel, handed her husband a bottle of red wine then sat across from Simone.

"Mon meilleur — Bordeaux." Leon held the bottle before Simone. "Spécialement pour vous."

"Merci beaucoup." She smiled, honored that he was presenting her with his "best wine."

He filled their glasses then lifted his in a toast. "À Simone, j'espère une cousine de loin." He smiled warmly at her.

"He says he hopes you are a cousin from afar," Noel explained, although she'd gotten the gist of it. She thanked Leon in French then took a sip, and although she knew nothing about wine, she complimented him on his selection. Then he began to talk about the Beaumont family and question her about her relatives, but he was speaking so quickly that, once again, she felt lost. She apologized for her lacking language skills and turned to Noel for help.

"Leon tells you his papa is Andre Beaumont. Andre start this restaurant forty years ago but he retires now. Andre's papa, Leon's grandpapa, was Basile Beaumont. But he is gone."

"I wonder how old Basile would be . . . my great-grandmamma has passed on too, but she would've been ninety-five now. She's the one from Avre."

She watched as Noel translated this for Leon. Rubbing his chin, he nodded then told Noel a number and asked another question.

"Leon says his great-grandpapa was twenty-three when killed in World War II. His papa was infant. Leon wants to know when your great-grandmamma left Avre. And where did she go, and why did she go?"

So Simone relayed the story of her great-grandfather's plane being shot down in World War II, and how the two fell in love. Meanwhile Noel translated.

Suddenly Leon leaped to his feet and, pointing to his head, declared, "I know — I know" in French. Speaking with excitement, he announced he heard this story as a child. Before Noel could speak — since Simone understood Leon's meaning — she asked him to explain what story he referred to. So with Noel's help, Leon told the tale of an American pilot who was shot down and how his great-great-aunt found him and took him home to nurse the wounded man to health.

In broken French, Simone asked Leon the aunt's name, fully expecting him to answer, "Simone Sophia Beaumont."

"Tante Estelle!" he proclaimed happily. "Estelle Marie Beaumont."

Simone tried to hide her disappointment. "Oh."

"That is not your great-grandmamma?" Noel asked her.

"No." She shook her head. "And my great-grandfather was not a pilot. He was a navigator."

Leon was talking again, so Noel translated to explain that Leon's aunt still lived in Avre. "Estelle is ninety-one years old, the matriarch of the family."

"Ninety-one?" Simone considered this. Could Estelle be Great-grandmamma's sister? She'd never heard mention of a sister. But then she'd never heard mention of any family. "Ask Leon if there were any other World War II airmen rescued. Does he know of other stories?"

As Noel made this inquiry, Simone knew this was silly to ask. If a Beaumont had rescued an airman — in such a small town — it was most likely her great-grandfather.

"Leon does not know other stories. Just his Tante Estelle's story. It is a legend in his family."

"Does he know what became of the man she rescued?" Simone asked, watching as Noel translated.

Leon shook his head. And then Nicole stood, announcing it was time to serve dinner. After she and Leon left, Noel asked Simone if she was disappointed.

"No," she told him. "In fact, it seems likely that Leon's aunt must somehow be connected to my great-grandmamma. Even though my great-grandpapa wasn't a pilot, he might've been mistaken as one. And since Estelle's name is Beaumont, she might be a relative of my great-grandmamma. Can you ask Leon if it's possible for me to meet this woman?"

Noel agreed to do this, and as delectable dishes of food were brought out, he asked if this meeting could be arranged. Leon eagerly nodded, promising that he would personally take Simone to see his aunt tomorrow.

"Leon says morning is best for him — and for his aunt as well. Is ten o'clock good for you?"

"Perfect," she assured him. Then, feeling that she'd really made progress tonight, Simone focused her attention on the lovely meal and her generous hosts. With Noel's help, she got to know them better, discovering they'd been married almost fifteen years and were about the same age as Simone. Nicole, through Noel, asked about Simone's marital status.

"Never married," Simone confessed. Nicole expressed surprise, saying that Simone was too pretty not to have been married. Simone thanked her then explained about being raised by her grandmother and how she got ill. "I had to help her," she told them. "I guess I just never had time to get into a serious relationship." She knew she could've told them more. About Doctor Jonathan. Or even about her college beau and how he broke her heart. But it just seemed like too much.

Nicole nudged Noel with her elbow, saying something quietly, causing the three of them to laugh.

"Sorry," Noel told Simone. "Nicole suggests I get to know you better. My friends do not like that I am bachelor."

"I have friends like that too." Simone laughed. "I know just how you feel."

As the four of them ate and visited, Simone thought how nice it was to be with interesting people her own age . . . possibly relatives even. And when the evening finally came to an end, she thanked her hosts in her best French, honestly telling them that she'd never enjoyed a meal more.

Before she left, Leon promised to pick her up at the hotel in the morning.

"He says you're going to love his Tante Estelle," Noel translated. "She is a dear, sweet lady."

"I can't wait," she told them, thanking them again.

Simone dressed carefully in the morning. She wanted to make a good impression with Estelle Beaumont, even if it turned out she was only a distant cousin or not related at all. Waiting nervously by the fireplace in the lobby, she visited with Noel.

"Have you need of translation help?" he asked when it was nearly ten.

"Can you spare the time?" she asked hopefully.

"Oui. I am your servant."

She smiled gratefully. "Merci beaucoup!"

As Leon drove them through the snowy town, Noel and he chattered in French. Simone tried to make sense of it, catching a word here and there, but for the most part, it went right over her head. She partly blamed it on how nervous she felt. Not so much because she was about to meet a possible relative, but because she was thinking about her great-grandmother's treasure. Could it possibly be real?

Leon pulled up in front of a tall stone house, announcing this was his aunt's home. At least, that was what Simone thought he said. But as he parked and got out, she knew it must be right. The handsome house had a recently shoveled path, lined with rounded, snow-covered hedges. Beside the big wooden front door were rows of tall windows, with a Christmas tree showing through one. She praised the house as she got out of the car. "Très belle maison."

"Merci beaucoup pour Estelle." Leon grinned at her.

"Did Leon let his aunt know I was coming?" Simone quietly asked Noel as they crunched through the thin crust of snow. Noel spoke to Leon then relayed that the aunt was expecting only her nephew. "You are to be Leon's surprise."

"Oh?" She hoped it'd be a good surprise.

A middle-aged woman answered the door, welcoming Leon inside but frowning slightly as Noel and Simone stepped into the elegant foyer. Simone took in the marble floor, intricately carved staircase, and impressive antique grandfather clock. As they removed their coats, Leon explained that he'd brought guests. The woman, who appeared to be the housekeeper, took their coats then led them to a parlor where a table of tea things was nicely set — for two. A petite, white-haired woman was already seated at the table, but gazing curiously at Simone through wire-rimmed glasses, she seemed somewhat bewildered. "Bonjour?" She peered at her nephew.

"Bonjour, Tante Estelle." Leon leaned down to kiss both her cheeks, quickly explaining he'd brought friends. Simone smiled nervously as Noel quietly translated and Estelle called out to her housekeeper, telling Willa to bring more teacups and another plate of pastries. Meanwhile Leon pulled two more chairs to the table.

"Asseyez-vous." Estelle quietly commanded them to sit then turned back to Leon. "Présente-les, s'il te plaît."

Simone knew she was requesting a proper introduction, and complying with her, Leon introduced Noel Durand as the innkeeper of Chateau Edelweiss and Simone Winthrop as his new friend. Unless Simone was mistaken, the old woman's pale eyebrows arched upon hearing her name. Leon began to pour tea for everyone, chatting happily at his aunt about Christmas plans, his café, and wife Nicole, but the whole while Estelle's eyes remained fixed on Simone.

Using her best French, Simone thanked their hostess for her hospitality and apologized for her lack of linguistic skills. Estelle somberly nodded then reached for her teacup. Feeling more uneasy, Simone did likewise. Estelle was clearly bothered by something. Quite likely her unexpected guests. The old woman's teacup rattled as she set it down and, turning to Leon, she asked him a question.

"She demands to know why Leon brought you here," Noel quietly interpreted with a furrowed brow. Perhaps he felt the tension too. As Leon answered his aunt, Noel continued to translate. "He's telling her that you're an American . . . that you came to Avre to search for family . . . and that your family name is Beaumont."

Lifting her teacup in midair, Estelle turned to Simone with a startled expression. "Beaumont?" she exclaimed.

"Oui," Simone answered calmly. "Mon arrière-grand-mère est Simone Sophia Beaumont."

Estelle scowled darkly. Setting her teacup back in her saucer with a loud clang, she reached for the cane that was leaning against her chair. Turning to Leon, she spoke in angry French, shaking her cane for emphasis. Noel, instead of translating, simply watched the startling scene with wide eyes.

"Tante Estelle," Leon said, interrupting her tirade of words. "Excusez-moi, s'il vous plaît." He turned to Noel, quietly explaining something as he got to his feet.

"We should go now," Noel told Simone as he quickly stood. "Leon's aunt is unwell."

"Je suis désolé." Simone apologized in French, adding that she hoped she would get well soon, then laid down her napkin and pushed back her chair.

"Bon débarras," Estelle growled, still clutching her cane and glaring as Simone stood up.

Unless Simone was mistaken, Estelle had just said "Good riddance." Feeling slightly shaky and rudely dismissed, Simone started backing away. "Au revoir, Madame Beaumont."

The three of them rushed out of the

parlor, hurriedly pulling on their coats and making a hasty exit. Once in the car, Simone questioned Leon about the abruptly ended tea party. After Leon spoke his piece, Noel attempted to translate.

"It seems Leon's aunt believes she was tricked, and she was not happy about it. She says Simone Sophia Beaumont is no relative of hers. But Leon is not so sure this is true. He has never seen his aunt act so rudely. He is confused by all this. He says his aunt is not herself today."

"Please, tell Leon I'm terribly sorry for having caused him so much trouble." Simone tugged on her gloves, wondering why on earth Estelle Beaumont was so disturbed by their visit. Was she really unwell? Or perhaps just mentally unstable. But she didn't want to ask Leon about that. She already felt guilty enough for the way this had turned out. All that fuss and they never even got to ask Leon's aunt about the American pilot she'd rescued.

Perhaps coming to Avre had been a mistake. As Leon drove them back to the hotel, Simone gazed out the window, trying to distract herself with the charmingly decorated homes and businesses. Everything in the small town looked so festive and bright for Christmas. Not in the gaudy way that some Californians liked, but more thoughtfully and, in her opinion, more beautifully.

But seeing these sweet homes with children playing outside and people visiting on doorsteps or shoveling snow only made her feel more like an outsider. Being on her own for the holidays suddenly felt gloomier than ever. From what she could see, Christmas was going to be cold and lonely here in Avre.

CHAPTER 8

At the hotel, Simone thanked Leon and Noel for their help and, not wanting to discuss the weird morning meeting further, jumped out of the car and hurried up to her room. She still couldn't make heads or tails of what had happened at the handsome stone house. Clearly, Estelle Beaumont had some sort of connection to Simone's great-grandmother. Apparently, a bad connection.

For a while, Simone paced back and forth in her room, trying to decide her next course of action. Part of her wanted to call it quits and just go home in time for Christmas. Hopefully Andrea wouldn't be too disappointed in her . . . and hopefully she'd put Simone up until she found a more permanent place to live. Yes, going home was probably the sensible thing to do.

Yet another part of her had become even more curious about her family heritage. Possibly due to Estelle's strong reaction. And, she reminded herself, Estelle was not the only Beaumont in town. For all Simone knew, Estelle might simply be a distant cousin caught up in some old family feud. Or maybe she wasn't a relative at all. In fact, it seemed likely that Beaumont could be her married name. Why hadn't Simone thought to ask about that?

Whatever the case, Simone decided she wouldn't allow grouchy old Estelle Beaumont to ruin her visit in Avre. It was too soon to give up. Realizing she'd skipped breakfast and was hungry for some good French food, she set out to explore the town a bit and hopefully find a good lunch spot. As she walked through town, she considered returning to Café Bleu, but not eager to face Leon quite yet, she decided to poke around a bit more instead.

After discovering a delightful restaurant, she spent the rest of the afternoon exploring Avre. By the time she headed back to the hotel, she no longer felt like such an outsider. In fact, it was almost as if the town was welcoming her . . . as if it was inviting her to make herself at home. Maybe it was the spirit of her great-grandmamma — happy to have her descendant in her hometown. Or maybe there was something deep inside Simone that connected with the French people. But conversing with shop-keepers and locals seemed to be getting easier.

It was just getting dusky as she reached the hotel. Chilled from trudging around in the snow, she eagerly entered the lobby. Hoping to soak up some of the heat, she hurried over to the crackling fireplace.

"Bonsoir!"

She looked over to the source of the greeting and realized that Noel was putting a big Christmas tree into place. "Bonsoir!" she called back.

"What do you think?" He waved to the tall evergreen.

"C'est beau!" she said excitedly. "But a bit crooked." She pointed to how it tilted to the left.

"Merci!" he called over his shoulder as he adjusted. "How is that?"

"Perfect." She nodded approval.

"It is my responsibility to get the tree up." He brushed off his hands. "Because I am the Christmas boy."

"Christmas boy?" Then she remembered his name. "*Noël?* That's French for Christmas. Does that mean you were born at Christmastime?"

"Oui. Three days before Christmas."

"Aha."

"So ever since I was a boy, it was my job to help get the tree."

"Will you decorate it?"

"No, no." He shook his head. "That is only for Maman. She likes it just so."

Simone laughed. "A perfectionist."

"Oui. You have met her?"

"No, but my grandma was like that. She liked to have things just so." She moved closer to the fireplace, warming her hands.

"Your great-grandmamma Simone Beaumont?"

"No. I mean my grandmother. Although she was more like a mother to me. She was a perfectionist. Well, until she became ill and . . . forgetful. But it was because she had Alzheimer's. She passed away. . . ."

"Oh, I am sorry for your loss. Is this why you seek your relations?"

She unbuttoned her coat to allow more heat in. "Sort of . . . I suppose."

He held up a finger. "Now I remember — I have news from Leon. He is sorry about his aunt. He does not know why she became angry. He has another plan."

"Oh?"

"His uncle, Arnou Beaumont. Leon will call and tell him about you . . . if you are interested to meet him."

"Yes. Very interested. Thank you." She frowned. "Well, unless this uncle is married to Estelle."

"No, no. Leon says his aunt is spinster. The oldest member of family. Arnou is her younger brother. He lives in country but comes to town on Wednesdays."

"That's tomorrow?"

"Oui. If you like, I will call Leon and ask him to arrange this meeting tomorrow."

"I'd like that. Well, as long as he's nothing like his older sister." She cringed to remember the disappointing tea party.

"I have met Arnou Beaumont before. A good man." Noel scratched his head. "Morning is best time for me. New guests arrive tomorrow afternoon."

"Morning is great." She smiled.

"I will let you know what time after I speak to Leon."

"Thank you so much."

"Have you a plan for dinner?" His pale brows arched hopefully.

"I had a late lunch at Bistro Enzo. Very nice." She held up a shopping bag. "And then I found Boulangerie Adrienne and picked up some bread and fruit and cheese as well as a few other provisions, so I think I'll be fine. Thank you."

Noel looked disappointed, but politely

tipped his head. She told him good night and went up to her room. It wasn't that she wouldn't have enjoyed going to dinner with him again, but she didn't want to give him the wrong idea. Certainly, he was a nice guy . . . but not someone she felt like dating. Still, his attention was flattering.

At ten o'clock the following morning, Noel drove Simone across town and parked in front of a red brick building. The sign above the door read FABRIQUE D'HORLOGE ET MONTRE D'AVRE. "*Horloge* means clock, right?" she asked Noel as they got out of the car.

"Oui. This is Avre Clock and Watch Factory."

"And this is where we're meeting Arnou Beaumont?"

"Oui. I did not know this before, but Leon say the Beaumont family owns the factory."

"Interesting." She waited as he opened the front door for her, but all she could think about was Kyle the clockmaker. Wouldn't a place like this be of interest to him? And yet he'd never called. For all she knew, he was still in Oslo. Best to put him out of her mind.

They were barely inside the shadowy factory when they were greeted by an elderly man with a full white beard. "Bienvenue." He welcomed them and, reaching out to Simone, warmly clasped her hand in both of his. "Je suis Oncle Arnou," he told her.

"Je m'appelle Simone Sophia Winthrop," she said with wide eyes. Was this sweet old man really her uncle?

Suddenly Oncle Arnou was speaking in rapid French — only some of which she could make out, including the name Simone Sophia and then the words *sœur aînée* which she knew meant "older sister."

Noel grabbed her arm. "He says Simone Sophia is his beloved older sister. He wants to know how she is and if she sent you."

Simone told him the condensed story of her great-grandmamma's life in America. "It was her dying wish that I come to Avre." She waited as Noel translated all this, watching as Oncle Arnou responded with sympathy.

"He says Simone Sophia was his favorite sister as a young child. She was ten years older, and he was only eight when she married the pilot."

Still, excited about her newfound relative, Simone explained that her great-grandfather had been a navigator — not a pilot — but that he'd also passed away. Oncle Arnou questioned her about other family members, and she told him about her grandfather and how he died in a plane wreck and also about her mother, confessing she did not know her whereabouts. Again, Oncle Arnou expressed his regrets. As he called out to a man passing by, Simone felt like pinching herself. This was all truly happening — she was meeting actual relatives!

"That is Arnou's son," Noel said, gesturing toward a man in his sixties. And now she was introduced to her cousin Emile. He, too, appeared happy to meet her. So unlike yesterday's encounter with the woman she now knew as Tante Estelle and her great-grandmamma's younger sister.

"Emile and Arnou wish you to see the factory," Noel told her. "Do you want to tour?"

"Yes, of course." She eagerly agreed.

Her two relatives proudly led them into another section of the factory. Here, numerous stations were set up with a lot of interesting-looking tools and parts and clock and watch pieces. The two men took turns explaining how the factory was originally established by a watchmaker from Geneva, Switzerland, which was only about twenty miles away from Avre.

"When the clock company was about a hundred years old, the owners wanted to close the factory. Right after the war . . .

clocks not selling. Employees worried for jobs. Especially your aunt." Noel paused to listen to Oncle Arnou then turned to Simone with a surprised expression. "He says Estelle bought the factory. The Beaumont family has owned it for about seventy-five years." He blinked. "I did not know this."

"Interesting that a woman — back then — would buy a business like this," said Simone. "I wonder why she wanted to own a clock and watch factory."

Noel asked Oncle Arnou then nodded. "Your aunt worked here during the war. She loved her work and didn't want to see the factory closed."

"Oh." She absorbed this information. Apparently her cantankerous spinster aunt had been an enterprising businesswoman. And judging by her lovely home, she had been successful too.

Simone paused by a workstation where an elderly artist was putting his touches on a clockface. His hand trembled slightly as he held the brush, but the strokes were smooth. She complimented him in French, and he turned to thank her. Then through Noel's interpretation, he told her he was very old. "He says his wife wants him to retire."

Simone smiled, wishing the old man well. Instead of responding, he spoke of another relative, pointing toward the other end of the workroom.

"Oncle Arnou wants you to meet his granddaughter — your cousin," Noel continued to translate as they followed her uncle. "She's Emile's younger daughter. He has two girls, but the older lives in Avignon." As they passed a few more workstations, Simone learned how Oncle Arnou's two brothers, both older than Simone, had died in the war. "Arnou was the first Beaumont, after Estelle, to work here in the factory. He ran the company for thirty years and then Emile took over. Arnou hopes Sylvie will be next." Noel lowered his voice. "Although her papa is uncertain. Emile just said Sylvie does not like the clock and watch business."

Simone tried to sort out and absorb all this family information as Emile opened a door that read office. It was a lot to take in. And yet it was thrilling to learn of all these relatives. Oncle Arnou, Cousin Emile, and his daughter Sylvie. And, of course, there was Tante Estelle. Although Simone didn't care to think about that right now.

Oncle Arnou waved Simone into the business office, calling out to his granddaughter and inviting her to come meet her American cousin.

"Sylvie parle anglais," Emile proudly told Simone, adding that she'd attended university.

Simone felt relieved that at least one family member spoke English. But before she could respond, she saw something that literally took her breath away. "Kyle?" Her jaw dropped as she stared at the same dark-haired man who'd helped her on the transatlantic flight. "Is that you?"

"Simone!" he exclaimed. With a wide grin, he rushed over to meet her. On his heels was a blonde woman, who curiously watched as the two embraced.

"Is this real?" Simone asked as they stepped apart.

"Unbelievably real." Kyle laughed. Suddenly everyone was talking at once. In the mix of French and English, Simone made two key discoveries. The pretty blonde was her cousin Sylvie, and Kyle was here to discuss an apprenticeship. She also learned that Kyle had tried to call her in Paris but seemed to have gotten the wrong number.

"You two are acquainted?" Sylvie asked, her blue eyes wide. "Did you know you would meet here in Avre?"

"I had no idea Simone was coming to Avre," Kyle told her. "We met on the plane."

"So you are not old friends?" Sylvie asked.

"Not at all," Simone assured her.

Sylvie looked doubtful. "And you are truly my cousin?"

Simone explained about her great-grandmamma and namesake Simone Sophia and then Oncle Arnou took over, excitedly telling Sylvie about his older sister who'd married an American. But instead of focusing on her wonderful newfound family, Simone couldn't take her eyes off Kyle. How was this even possible? Was she dreaming?

CHAPTER 9

More than anything, Simone wanted to be alone with Kyle. She wanted to hear about his time in Norway and update him on her own adventures. But since Sylvie had scheduled the whole day for him at the factory — a gesture that, according to Kyle, was quite generous — Simone knew he couldn't get away.

"I'll call you as soon as we're done here," he'd promised. This time she made certain he got the right number and her full name. And just to be safe, she got his number as well. But before they parted ways, Oncle Arnou began planning a celebratory family dinner for the same evening, insisting that Kyle and Noel must come as well and that he would ask Leon and Nicole to cater the affair.

Simone gratefully agreed to come, but when Oncle Arnou announced they would hold the festive dinner at Tante Estelle's house, she wasn't so sure. Exchanging glances with Noel, she knew he questioned the location as well. He even asked her uncle if he was sure his elderly sister would approve of these plans, but Oncle Arnou just waved him off.

"Arnou says she often hosts relatives in the family home," Noel quietly told Simone. "The house has room for a crowd."

That didn't really address her concerns, but maybe it didn't matter. Somehow with Kyle here, it felt similar to flying in a plane; she could face anything. Even her cranky old aunt!

By the time Kyle called Simone, it was past five. He apologized, explaining how Sylvie made certain he saw every aspect of the clockmaking business. "It was educational and a great opportunity to see the ins and outs of the factory, but all the while I kept thinking about sneaking off to see you. I still can't believe you're here. Or that you're related to the owners of the clock and watch company."

Simone laughed. "I'm surprised too. I can't wait to catch up with you. I want to tell you about my time in Paris, and I want to hear how it went in Norway. How long do you expect to be in Avre?"

"To be honest, I thought I was just passing through. I planned to be on the train for Geneva right now."

"I'm so glad you're not. I hope you are too."

"Absolutely."

"What caused you to change your plans?" Simone hoped he was going to say it was because of her.

"Sylvie," he declared, bursting her bubble. "You see, when I first spoke to her — that was on the phone on Monday when I called from Paris — I explained my plans to come through Avre. I told her I was looking for an apprenticeship, but she told me it was impossible. So I asked about a quick tour of the company, and she said they didn't do tours. Then I explained about my friend Claude —"

"Your old clockmaker neighbor?"

"Yes. You *were* listening."

"Of course."

"Anyway, I told Sylvie how Claude had worked at the Avre factory back before World War II, and she agreed to a short tour."

"A short tour? You were there all day."

"I know. Sylvie seemed to change her mind after she finished with the short tour. That ended right before you showed up.

When you walked in, Sylvie was actually talking to me about an apprenticeship."

For some reason Simone wondered if Sylvie really wanted an apprentice . . . or something more. But, feeling guilty for her suspicions, she tried to dismiss the idea. "Wow, you must've really won her over."

"I guess so. All in all, this has been a pretty good day for me. But how about you?" he asked. "Any luck with your treasure hunt?"

She told him about her contrary aunt. "But you'll get to meet her tonight."

"Speaking of that. I don't have a car since I'm traveling by train, but Sylvie offered a ride to her aunt's house. I'll bet we could pick you up."

"Well, since Noel plans to go, I might as well ride with him."

"Right. I noticed he speaks pretty good English. How did you guys meet?"

"Noel's family owns the inn where I'm a guest. He's helped me with some translation issues. Where are you staying?"

"A guesthouse that Sylvie recommended. But it's got paper-thin walls and feels pretty drafty. Do you think Noel's place has a vacancy?"

"You should ask him." She described her room and the lobby and fireplace. "There's even a Christmas tree. The place is quite charming. I give it five stars." Naturally, she wouldn't mind having Kyle nearby, especially since she still suspected Cousin Sylvie had more than just a passing interest in him. And perhaps it was in the back of her mind as she selected an outfit for the family dinner.

In a flowing skirt, vintage lace top, and stylish boots, she felt chic, feminine, and pretty as she went downstairs to the lobby. And when Noel's eyes lit up, she could tell he approved. Hopefully Kyle would too.

"Sorry to keep you waiting," she told Noel as they went outside into the crisp evening air.

"Not a problem." He opened the car door for her, waiting for her to get inside. "Are you uneasy about seeing Estelle?"

"Oui." She didn't care to admit that her aunt was the main reason she'd dillydallied upstairs at the inn. She didn't want to be the first to arrive. Hopefully with others around, Tante Estelle would be on better behavior.

"I cannot comprehend why Estelle dislikes you, Simone, especially now we know you are her relation."

"Maybe *that* is why," Simone said. "I suspect she was not fond of my great-grandmamma."

"Aha. I think I understand your meaning."

Noel chattered pleasantly as he drove through town, but the only two things on Simone's mind were seeing Kyle again and trying to figure out Tante Estelle.

As before, it was the housekeeper Willa who answered the front door, only this time more formally attired in a plain black dress and apron. She smiled politely at Noel but narrowed her eyes ever so slightly at Simone as she took their coats.

"Bienvenue!" Oncle Arnou welcomed them both into the house, explaining through Noel that the family was gathered in the parlor as he led them toward the sounds of voices. The room was crowded with more than a dozen people, some Simone knew and some she did not. But everyone grew quiet as she came in, and Oncle Arnou, assisted by Sylvie, performed introductions. All the while Tante Estelle remained in her wingback chair. Wearing a plum-colored dress and with every white hair in place, she possessed an air of royalty gazing upon her subjects with approval. Except for Simone. Again, Estelle seemed to view her great-great-niece with great, great disdain.

With introductions complete, Simone

tried to act as if she felt no scrutinizing disapproval from Tante Estelle. Instead, with Noel's help, she engaged Oncle Arnou's wife, Yvette, in conversation. The elderly woman was warm and sweet and very curious about her new American relative. As they visited, Simone couldn't help but notice how Sylvie and Kyle appeared to be in Tante Estelle's good graces. Catching snippets of conversation, Simone could tell that her unpredictable aunt was impressed with Kyle's interest in clockmaking.

At dinnertime Estelle, with her cane in hand, led everyone into a large dining room where she was seated at the head of a long, elegantly set table. Still acting like the Queen Mother, she insisted Sylvie and Kyle sit to her right and left. Meanwhile, Oncle Arnou occupied the opposite end with his wife and Simone on either side, and the others, still chattering pleasantly, filled the remaining chairs.

So far, Tante Estelle hadn't uttered more than a crisp bonsoir to Simone. And Kyle, preoccupied with Sylvie, hadn't said much more. Simone tried to conceal her disappointment during dinner. Fortunately Noel, seated beside her and helpfully interpreting, managed to keep their end of the table conversing nicely. For this, she was grateful.

After a delicious meal, the group migrated back to the parlor as well as a den-like room where Estelle offered port, fruit, and cheese. By now Simone had gleaned enough information from Oncle Arnou to know this house had once been her great-grandmamma's home, and when he offered her the full tour, she eagerly accepted. With Noel accompanying them as translator, she had opportunity to question her uncle without the other family members overhearing the conversation.

He started the tour on the first floor. It seemed that Estelle, because of a skiing accident that had injured her hip as a young adult, only occupied this level. He showed them the master bedroom, which Estelle had utilized since their father's death. Next he opened the door to a large "modernized" bathroom. This had been his room as a young child.

"He says he was the baby of the family — a surprise to his older parents," Noel said. "But his mother was in bad health. She died when he was still very small."

As Oncle Arnou led them upstairs, he explained how his four older siblings had stayed on the second floor. His older brothers, Jean and Basile, shared the largest bedroom — and he had looked forward to moving up there someday. But then the war came. . . . Jean and Basile, both in their twenties, went into the army and never came home. As Oncle Arnou opened the door to the boys' room, Simone recalled Leon mentioning that his Grandpapa Basile had died in the war. So this had been his room.

"Arnou says he never could be in that room after losing his brothers," Noel quietly repeated.

Simone expressed her sincere regrets, patting Oncle Arnou on the back. She understood loneliness too. "This seems a lovely spare room," she added, hoping to change to a happier subject. She went around the room, admiring the fine furnishings and the large bay window. As he closed the door, Oncle Arnou admitted that it was used for guests . . . sometimes. Next he showed them a small Spartan room with only a bed, dresser, and chair, explaining it was once Estelle's room but was now used by Willa.

Finally, he showed them where his oldest sister had spent her youth. "Simone Sophia." He sighed again, expressing how much he had loved her and how kind she had been to him. Like a second mother.

Simone asked her uncle if this was how the room looked when his sister lived here so long ago. He nodded somberly, saying nothing had changed — that after Simone went to America, only he and Estelle and their grieving father remained in this big house . . . and that it became sad and quiet.

As Simone looked around the room, which must've been pretty at one time but now looked dusty and faded, she couldn't help but wonder about the treasure Great-grandmamma had written about in her letter. Was it possibly still in here somewhere? This room did seem almost frozen in time . . . as if the young Simone Sophia had just packed her bag and departed.

Simone traced a finger through the dust, longing to go through the bureau drawers, or to search through the armoire and peek under the bed. Of course, she wouldn't dare. Instead, she gazed at the pictures on the walls — an ornately framed print of a shepherd girl, another framed print of three handsome hunting dogs, and a more simply framed black-and-white photo of, Simone guessed, her great-grandmamma as a teen with a girlfriend. Simone stared in wonder. She'd always known that she resembled her namesake, but this photo — with her great-grandmamma's curls blowing wildly in the wind — was uncannily familiar.

Hearing Oncle Arnou clear his throat,

Simone suspected her tour was over. She thanked him and reluctantly left the room. Then noticing another door, she asked where it led and was informed it was an attic — only for storage. They were just about to go down the stairs when she heard voices and someone coming up toward them.

"Oh, there you are," Kyle said as he and Sylvie paused on the landing. "I hoped you hadn't left yet."

"Oncle Arnou was just giving me a tour." Simone smiled brightly, trying to ignore the observation that Sylvie's arm was looped through Kyle's.

"Sylvie is showing me the spare room," Kyle said. "Tante Estelle has graciously invited me to be her guest."

"Here in this house?" Simone experienced a double-edged pang of jealousy. Her aunt was extending hospitality to Kyle when he wasn't even a relative? And Sylvie seemed to be smugly pleased about it.

"Yes. I hear there is a nice guest room up here."

"I just saw it." Simone forced a smile. "It looks comfortable."

"Oh, it is," Sylvie assured her. "Come, Kyle. It is right this way."

Seeing no reason to remain, Simone headed for the stairs. She knew it was childish to feel so envious, but she couldn't seem to help it. Now she really did want to leave this place. Once they were back on the main floor, she thanked Oncle Arnou and then, not wanting to feel Tante Estelle's scorn one more time or to create a scene, made an excuse that was partially true.

"I, uh, I don't feel very well." She waited for Noel to translate. "Please, make my excuses to your family. I'd like to go now. Bonsoir."

Oncle Arnou looked disappointed but sympathetic as he patted her on the shoulder, telling her to get well and then, as Noel helped Simone into her coat, Oncle Arnou said something about Christmas, but Simone couldn't quite get the gist of it.

"He wants to know if you will still be in Avre for Christmas," Noel translated. "He wants you to join his family for their annual festivities."

Simone brightened, smiling at her uncle. "Oui. Très bien. Merci beaucoup!"

Oncle Arnou beamed at her, promising to be in touch about it soon. "Bonsoir!"

After they were outside, Noel seemed concerned for her health. Taking her arm and warning of the icy walk, he helped her out to the car. Once inside, she confessed she wasn't really ill. "I guess I'm just sad."

"Because of Estelle?"

She nodded. "I think she hates me."

"Hate is a strong word." He sighed. "But dislike perhaps?"

She couldn't help but smile. "Yes. She definitely dislikes me." But she certainly seemed to like Kyle . . . as did Sylvie.

CHAPTER 10

The next morning, Simone felt torn. On one hand, she was ready to march over to Tante Estelle's house and demand to know the meaning of her inhospitable treatment. On the other hand, she wanted to just forget the whole thing and catch the next train to Paris. As sweet and tempting as Oncle Arnou's invitation to spend Christmas with him and his family was, she realized that meant his older sister would be there too. And the idea of spending Christmas with that mean-spirited woman hostilely glaring at her . . . well, it was not particularly enticing. It didn't help that Kyle seemed to be welcomed with open arms. Both Tante Estelle's and Sylvie's.

Feeling disgruntled, Simone went downstairs to partake in the continental breakfast that Noel's mother set out each morning. So far, Simone had only had it once, but it had been good. With a soft-boiled egg, buttery croissant, and hot black coffee, she sat down at one of the little tables and proceeded to eat. Several other couples were eating breakfast as well and clearly, the inn was getting busier. Which probably meant Noel was getting busier too, and her idea of asking him to take her to visit Tante Estelle — and translate — was probably out. Probably for the best. Simone needed to confront her cantankerous aunt with a cool head. And that might take time.

After her breakfast, Simone bundled up with the intent to walk to town and do some more exploring and shopping but was barely down the street when it began to snow so hard she could barely see. She hurried back, deciding this was a good day to remain indoors. Maybe she'd pull out her sketch pad or simply snuggle up with a book and forget the rest of the world for a while. *Que sera, sera.*

It was midafternoon when her phone jangled. Expecting it might be Noel, she was surprised to see it was Kyle. "Are you okay?" he asked with what seemed like concern in his voice. "Sylvie told me you got sick last night. I was going to call earlier but thought you might be resting."

"I'm fine." She stood to stretch, peering

out the window to see the blizzard had subsided for the moment. "Just having a stay-in day."

"Oh, good. I've been at the factory all day."

"How's that going?" She tried to sound more interested than she felt.

"Great. I'm already learning a lot."

"So, I assume that means you've actually begun your apprenticeship. Is Sylvie your teacher?" She hoped she didn't sound too probing.

"No. Sylvie doesn't seem to know much about clock or watchmaking."

"She doesn't?" Relief washed over her as she sat back down in the chair by the window.

"Her degree's in business administration. Her job at the factory is to keep things running like clockwork." He chuckled.

"Oh, yeah, I think Emile mentioned that. But he seemed concerned, like he doesn't expect her to remain in the family business." Okay, she knew she was fishing now, but she was curious.

"Really? I don't get that feeling. Sylvie seems to like it there."

"Oh, that's nice. Emile will be pleased."

"Anyway, I didn't call to talk about Sylvie. I thought if you were feeling better, maybe we could get together. We never really got to catch up much last night."

"Yeah, that'd be great. What did you have in mind?" She peered out the window to see dark heavy clouds coming down from the mountains. "I wanted to walk around town some but looks like we're in for more snow."

"I have Sylvie's car for the afternoon so that I can move my stuff from the guesthouse over to Tante Estelle's place," he said. "Want to come with me? Maybe afterward, we could get dinner?"

"That sounds great." Okay, the last part sounded great. She wasn't so sure about going to Tante Estelle's house again. But before she could change her mind, he said he was on his way.

As Simone went downstairs, she wasn't sure what made her more nervous. Being alone with Kyle . . . or crossing paths with her cranky aunt again. But seeing his smiling face as he came into the lobby made her forget all about Tante Estelle.

Kyle greeted Noel, who was checking in guests, then waved to Simone. "This does look like a nice inn." He paused to take in the fireplace and decorated tree. "Very cozy and welcoming."

"Maybe you'd like to change your mind

about staying with Tante Estelle?" she said in a teasing tone.

"No way." He firmly shook his head as they headed for the door. "For one thing, Noel already told me the inn's full up during the holidays. But besides that, my staying with your aunt will give you opportunity to poke around."

"Poke around?" She frowned.

"You know, for your treasure hunt."

She bit her lip. "Well, I'm not sure that will go over too well with my, uh, aunt. Didn't you notice how the old woman isn't overly fond of me?"

"I sort of got that message. But why?" He opened the passenger door to the little red car for her.

"I wish I knew."

After he got in, she told him about the first encounter with Tante Estelle. "She all but threw us out of her house."

"Weird. She seemed very nice to me."

"To *you.*" Simone sighed. "According to Oncle Arnou, Sylvie is her favorite niece. So, if Tante Estelle thinks you're involved with her, well, maybe that was your ticket into her secret society."

"Maybe. But she also appreciates that I'm a clockmaker. You know, she was a clock-maker as a young woman. It was rather unusual back then. And to buy the clock-making business, well, that was no small feat. I'd really like to hear more about that."

"So would I."

"Well, somehow we have to get you onto her good side, Simone."

"I thought about going directly to her and asking why she dislikes me so much," she admitted.

"The direct approach is usually best. But how about if we make a plan B — just in case she gives you the cold shoulder again."

"A plan B?"

"Yes. I thought I could occupy the old gal while you poke around upstairs. You could go up there on the pretext of taking my bags to my room while I'm caught up in conversation with her. She's expecting me for afternoon tea."

"Tea again." Simone groaned.

"So, anyway, if tea goes badly, you just excuse yourself for whatever reason. Or pretend to be my bellboy."

"Great. I'd love the chance to look around."

He turned on the wipers as snowflakes started to fall. "Sylvie showed me your great-grandmother's room last night. I was pretty stunned. I mean, it looked like something right out of a time warp. Like nothing had changed since World War II. Do you think the treasure might really be in there?"

"I kind of got that feeling." She felt a flush of excitement to imagine having the opportunity to search that room. "Oncle Arnou said Tante Estelle never goes upstairs because of her bad hip, so I assume it's just as my great-grandmamma left it."

"Sure looked that way to me. So, if Tante Estelle doesn't warm up to you, just slip away. I'll keep her busy by talking about clockmaking. I already told her I have lots of ideas and questions — and I really do. In the meantime, you can freely treasure hunt."

Simone hoped he was right, but she could also imagine her ancient aunt chasing her down with her cane and screaming wildly in French.

"Ready for this?" He grinned at her as he pulled up in front of the tall stone house.

"I guess. But I have no idea what I'm looking for."

"I'll take the lead with Tante Estelle," he said as they went up the walk. "I plan to act oblivious to her feelings toward you."

"And your French is better than mine," Simone said, "so I'll appreciate any help I can get."

"You got it." He rang the doorbell and,

just like real déjà vu, they were standing in the elegant foyer again. The grandfather clock was still ticking and Willa's expression — toward Simone — was still decidedly suspicious. As they were led to the parlor, where the tea table was set for two, Simone braced herself for another tirade. But before Tante Estelle could throw a fit, Kyle rushed over to greet her, warmly grasping her hand and complimenting her on last night's dinner party. Then he apologized for bringing an unexpected guest, adding that he thought she would be glad to have her niece join them.

Kyle continued to talk, almost as if he'd rehearsed the whole thing. Simone took in most of it since his accent was American, but some things slipped past her. Finally, he told a rather stunned Tante Estelle that Simone wanted to ask questions about her dearly departed older sister. And, unless Simone was mistaken, Tante Estelle's pale gray eyes grew a bit misty. She called out to Willa to bring more tea things and asked Kyle to get another chair.

Simone sat down, trying to get her bearings. She really wanted to ask Tante Estelle why she'd denied being related to her older sister and why she had been so rude to Simone but suspected that would backfire.

Instead, in her best French and with Kyle's help, she began to speak of her great-grandmamma. Hoping to garner some empathy, Simone explained how she missed having family since so many of her relatives had passed away.

Estelle began speaking in rapid French again, but not in an angry way this time. Kyle translated. "She says she has lived a lonely life too. She lost her mother at a young age and her older brothers in the war. Then her only sister left with the American pilot. And when she was only twenty-four, she lost her father. So she relates to you." His eyes brightened. "You have something in common."

Simone wondered why Tante Estelle had never married or had children of her own but felt it would be rude to ask. Instead, she spoke of her great-grandmamma again. "I knew she grew up here in Avre, by the French Alps, but she never spoke much of her family."

Tante Estelle nodded sadly as Kyle relayed this to her. And now feeling like she had her aunt's sympathy, Simone removed the letter from her bag. With Kyle's help, she read the letter, but before he could finish with his translation, Tante Estelle became enraged. Shaking her cane, she shrilly yelled, "Il n'y

136

a pas de trésor!" again and again, louder each time.

"She says there is no treasure," Kyle told Simone.

"I know. I got that." Simone stood, apologizing. "Excusez-moi, s'il vous plaît." She put the letter in her bag. "I'll bring in your bags for you," she told Kyle. "You stay and visit."

His eyes twinkled as she backed away. She knew he had plan B in mind as she went out to the car. Willa eyed Simone curiously when she returned with Kyle's bags, but Simone explained in choppy French that she was taking them to Kyle's room for him. Since it was a full load, the older housekeeper actually seemed relieved.

Simone set the bags in the guest room then tiptoed over to her great-grandmamma's bedroom, quietly slipping inside and closing the door. "Where is your treasure?" she whispered to the photo on the wall. Then setting her bag on the faded lilac bedspread, she started to explore. "Help me, Great-grandmamma. If you want me to find it, please, show me where to look . . . what I'm looking for."

At first she tried not to disturb things, but realizing that her tracks would clearly show in the disturbed dust, she began to search more freely. And as interesting as it was to find old pieces of vintage clothing, faded scarves, a pair of worn shoes, an old bottle of perfume, movie tickets, and various other mementos — things left behind in the rush to leave the country — she found nothing that resembled a true treasure. What if her original intuitions had been correct? What if there was no treasure? What if Great-grandmamma had simply experienced an elderly end-of-life moment?

Still, determined to do this right, Simone continued to search under the bed, under the rug, under the mattress, inside the pillow shams. She even examined a china doll in a faded lace dress, checking to see if perhaps the padded torso had been opened and restitched, but it seemed intact. She peeked behind the pictures on the wall to see if something, maybe a possible clue, was hidden there. Finally, she stood in the center of the room, shaking dust from her hands and trying to determine if she'd missed anything.

She was about to give up when she remembered a scene from an old movie where something had been hidden on top of an armoire. It seemed a long shot as she quietly moved a chair across the room, but she was determined to leave no stone unturned here. Who knew if she'd ever get another chance?

She climbed onto the chair and, reaching above the armoire and feeling around, she was stunned to touch what felt like a boxy item. She removed the piece to find a padded box, slightly bigger than a shoebox. She brushed off the dust to see the faded pink vinyl was embossed with a border of roses.

With a pounding heart and shaking hands, she climbed down from the chair and sat on it. Now almost afraid to breathe, she tried the brass latch that seemed to be broken. She slowly opened the box, but hearing the tinkling sounds of *Swan Lake,* she quickly closed it again.

Taking in another deep breath, she convinced herself it wasn't loud enough to be heard downstairs and lifted the lid again. The inside was lined with rose-colored velvet, and a tray popped up with the lid open. But the tray was empty. And other than a few small pieces of costume jewelry — trinkets a young girl might treasure and wear — there was nothing of value. Beneath a tarnished charm bracelet, she saw a slip of folded paper. Wondering if perhaps it held a clue, she read it. Only three words: "Je suis désolé" in faded blue ink, which Simone knew meant "I am sorry." But sorry for what?

Hearing a noise downstairs, she got nervous. Replacing the note in the jewelry box, she returned it to the spot above the armoire then quietly put the chair back. *I am sorry.* What was behind it? Did her great-grandmamma jot that down before fleeing with her American flyer? Her way of apologizing for abandoning her family during the war?

Simone vaguely wondered if it was meant for her. Of course, that made no sense. But she could imagine it was an apology for the fact that she'd gone on a wild-goose chase only to discover there had never been a treasure. *C'est la vie.*

CHAPTER 11

Because Kyle had to return Sylvie's car, they used a taxi to go to dinner. But after a delightful meal at Café Bleu and a fun visit over complimentary dessert with Leon and Nicole, Kyle asked Simone how she felt about walking.

"I know it's crisp out, but the sky's cleared up nicely," he said as they stepped out the door.

As she buttoned her coat, Simone gazed up at the starlit sky. "It's beautiful out here."

"And only half a mile to your inn." Kyle zipped his jacket. "I'll escort you safely there."

"I think that sounds lovely, but you'll still have a long walk back to Tante Estelle's house." She wrapped her scarf around her neck.

He shrugged as he took her hand. "After all that food, that extra couple of miles to Tante Estelle's house sounds good." So they set out. "Speaking of your aunt," he said, "I didn't bring it up in front of your cousins because I know it makes you uncomfortable, but I wanted to tell you what Tante Estelle said while you were upstairs sacking that bedroom."

"I didn't *sack* it." She chuckled. "Like I already said, the only thing out of place up there now is the dust. Not that anyone will notice."

"I wonder if Tante Estelle knows about the apology note you found. It wouldn't seem so weird except that it sounds like it was hidden. Probably since the war years."

"I know. I have some theories, but none of them feel quite right. But back to my contrary aunt. What did she say to you?"

"Well, she actually felt sorry for the way she treated you. But I think I know why she did."

"Why?" Simone turned to look at him in the lamplight.

"Because you remind her of her older sister. She says you look like her."

"Well, that's not news to me. I've seen pictures of her when she was young. They were in black and white, but Great-grandmamma told me her hair used to be wavy and auburn — just like mine."

"Your great-grandmamma must've been

very pretty." He squeezed her hand, and she felt her cheeks warming.

"Back to what you were saying — because I remind Tante Estelle of her sister, she hates me?" Simone asked.

"That's the feeling I got. She didn't say as much, but I suspect she was jealous of her older sister."

"Well, I guess I can imagine sibling rivalry while they were girls. But that was ages ago. Wouldn't she have gotten over it by now? And it seems she would've missed her sister. They were the only girls in the family."

"I don't know. But when I asked her about your great-grandmother — about how she left France with the American serviceman — she got very tight-lipped."

"It's like bad blood or something."

"Or something." He slowly shook his head. "So then I told her that she'd hurt your feelings."

"You did?" Simone was touched.

"And she actually seemed surprised. I honestly think she saw so much of her older sister in you that she practically forgot you were the great-granddaughter."

"As weird as that sounds, I kind of get it."

"And then she said she was sorry and that she hadn't meant to hurt you."

"Sure could've fooled me. I halfway expected her to take her cane to me."

He laughed. "Anyway, she said she's going to make things right with you."

"That'd be nice." Then Simone considered her elderly aunt's dark scowling face and sighed. "But I won't be holding my breath."

"Just keep your phone handy. I gave her your number, and she assured me she plans to call you tomorrow morning."

"Hopefully I'll be able to understand her. My French is improving, but I still get lost when people talk too fast. Like at dinner tonight, what was Leon saying about Sylvie that I missed?"

Kyle chuckled. "It was kind of a warning."

"A warning?" Simone glanced at him.

"He said his cousin can be unpredictable. He said she's been like that since childhood. She can run hot then cold. He compared her to your Tante Estelle."

"Interesting." Simone kept her thoughts to herself but felt relieved Leon had mentioned this to Kyle. It wasn't that she didn't trust Sylvie, but something about her relative made her uneasy — right from the start.

"Well, here we are." Kyle stopped in front of the inn.

"Come in and get warmed up before your

walk to Tante Estelle's."

"Don't mind if I do."

They were just taking the chill off in front of the big fireplace when Noel's mother came over to them. Glancing around the nearly empty lobby with a furtive glance, she greeted Simone, waiting as Simone introduced her to Kyle.

"Très bien." Madame Durand nodded then, speaking quietly, explained that Noel's thirty-fifth birthday was on Tuesday and she was hosting a surprise party, inviting them both to attend. They accepted her invitation, assuring her they would keep quiet about the celebration.

"Isn't she sweet," Simone said as the woman scurried away. "She and Noel bicker like crazy sometimes — and over the silliest things — but when it's all said and done, you can always tell how much they love each other."

"Maybe it's because the French are more open with their feelings." Kyle's eyes glowed warmly in the firelight, and he lowered his voice. "I suppose we could learn a thing or two from them."

Simone leaned in, certain he was about to kiss her, but just then a male voice interrupted, and they both turned to see Noel coming their way with a load of firewood in

145

his arms.

"Bonsoir," he said again as he cheerfully fed the fire. "This will help you warm." He stepped back, dusting off his sleeves with a broad smile on his face. "I did not interrupt anything?"

"No, no." Kyle rezipped his jacket. "I better get going. I have to be at work by eight tomorrow."

Simone thanked him and, watching him go, still wondered . . . was he about to kiss her or had she imagined it? Whatever the case, she planned to keep in mind what he'd said about the French not hiding their feelings. It didn't come naturally to her, but she would try to be more demonstrative . . . more French.

"You are lost in thought?" Noel asked quietly.

"Oh." She turned to see he was still there, seeming to study her. "I guess so."

"Are you troubled? Is it your aunt again?"

Glad for Tante Estelle as a segue, she described today's awkward visit to Noel. "But Kyle thinks she's going to call me tomorrow . . . to apologize." She frowned. "I just hope I can understand her on the phone. My French isn't so great, and she speaks so quickly at times, especially if she's upset."

"I am glad to help translate." He thought-fully rubbed his chin. "Maybe I drive you to her house? For this conversation — eye to eye is best."

"I agree." She eagerly nodded. "I would rather be face-to-face."

"Then I take you."

She felt a bit guilty. Already he'd been more than helpful. "You're sure you can spare the time?"

"I will make time." He politely tipped his head. "For you, Simone."

Simone thanked him, then feeling self-conscious and even more uneasy, she excused herself. She didn't want to lead him on. But then, as she went upstairs, she remembered what Kyle had just pointed out . . . how the French were more demonstrative. What seemed a romantic gesture from Noel might simply be his way. Perhaps she was silly to read anything more into it. After all, hadn't she witnessed him expressing himself like that with other females? Kyle hadn't been the only one to warm up to Sylvie at Tante Estelle's the other night. But then Sylvie could be rather charming when she wanted to be. In a way, Noel was no different.

For the fourth time in as many days, Simone

found herself on Tante Estelle's doorstep. But this time she didn't feel quite so nervous. For one thing, she had a vague idea as to what she could expect from her outspoken spinster aunt — since this woman truly did run hot and cold. But more importantly, it seemed her aunt wanted to make amends with her. At least, Simone hoped that was why she'd been summoned.

With Noel along to interpret, they were once again led into the parlor where a tea table was neatly set for *three* people. Progress! Simone smiled stiffly, greeting Tante Estelle in her best French as she sat down. Her aunt politely thanked them for coming and asked Simone to pour tea.

As Simone filled the delicate teacups, Estelle, with Noel's help, explained how much Simone reminded her of her older sister. "She says upon first seeing you, she was shocked. And then she was heartsick deep inside," Noel told Simone. "She did not know how to act." He paused to listen. "And now she is very sorry for her behaviors."

Simone assured her aunt that it was no problem and easily forgotten, then waited for her to continue. But then Tante Estelle began to talk so rapidly that Noel had to hold up his hands in order to relay her story to Simone. The woman looked teary-eyed as Noel explained how close she and her sister had been as children. A bit more than two years apart, they did everything together. Simone was a perfect older sister, and Estelle loved her and admired her greatly.

Simone smiled at her aunt, saying that she loved and admired her great-grandmamma too. Estelle eagerly nodded then continued to speak in warm tones, her gray eyes brightening as if remembering happier times.

Noel continued with interpreting. "She says Simone Sophia, she was the beauty of the family. Everyone admired her appearance. But Estelle, she was — how you say — not so beautiful. She was more adventurous. She would rather hike and ski and ride the horses than wear the pretty dresses."

"I'm kind of like that too," Simone said. "I like to be outdoors. I hike and ride my bike, but I've never skied. Although I'd like to try. Please, tell her I understand her." She waited as he conveyed this.

Estelle smiled. She told Simone about all the things she liked to do before the ski accident that crippled her hip. But then her words grew somber.

"She wants to know if you wish to hear

her story of the American flyer," Noel asked.

"Oh, oui. S'il vous plaît." Simone set down her teacup and leaned forward, watching closely as her aunt began her tale, gradually growing more animated, as if telling an adventure story. Then, pausing, she let Noel take over.

"She and friend, they go to hike in the hills — in springtime. It is wartime," he quickly relayed. "Estelle, she see broken plane pieces. She thinks is crash and wants to explore, but the friend, she is frightened — she run home. Estelle, she keeps walking. She discovers white parachute and then a man — with injuries. American flyer. Harold Winthrop."

Simone nodded. "Great-grandpapa. He was a navigator in the Army Air Corps and the only crew member to survive being shot down by the Germans."

He relayed this, waiting for her response. Estelle spoke quietly and with an expression that suggested she still worried, all these decades later, that her confession could land her in prison. Noel listened with wide eyes, making Simone even more impatient to hear what was being said.

"Estelle, she give Harold her knapsack and water, she promise to come back later," he said. "At home she make hiding place in the cellar. In this house. She fix bed and food and water. Before dark, Estelle, she return to the hills with splint and bandages. She sneaks Harold through town in darkness. Hides him in the cellar. He is her big secret. It is very exciting, no?"

"Yes. Very exciting," Simone agreed. "So she was the one who found my great-grandpapa. The one who rescued him. I always thought my great-grandmamma did that." Simone held up a finger. "But don't say that, Noel. Just tell her I'm very grateful she rescued him and that I think she was very brave. Especially for a young girl."

Estelle smiled and nodded, pausing to sip her tea and nibble a pastry. Her features seemed more relaxed now, as if relieved to have told this story. But Simone still had questions. "Ask her how my great-grandpapa met her sister."

As Estelle answered, her brow creased, and Simone knew it wasn't a happy part of her story. Noel made a sympathetic comment then explained to Simone about how the older sister discovered Harold in the cellar in early summer. "At first Estelle is upset and worried. But Simone Sophia promises to keep the secret. And she helps to move the wounded American up to the attic when all the family is gone one day. By

151

summer end he is well enough to leave. Estelle, she finds him old clothes to appear as French farmer. His hair, it is long, and he has full beard."

"Yes, I remember Great-grandmamma said he looked like an old man. She got him papers to pass over the borders and she dressed like an old farmer's wife."

After Noel relayed this to Estelle, her expression returned to the scowl she'd worn the past several days. As she spoke, her words grew angry.

Noel's brows arched with interest as he told Simone how upsetting it was for Estelle, and for their entire family. "No one knew that the American and Simone Sophia were in love and wanted to marry. No one expected Simone Sophia to go with him when he left. Everyone was shocked and saddened. Estelle says she was hurt deeply by her sister's betrayal. But it was love. It is what happened." Noel smiled at Simone then shrugged. "It is romantic, no?"

She nodded but felt a deep sadness for her aunt. Tante Estelle had never said as much, but Simone suspected that the fifteen-year-old younger sister — the French tomboy who'd rescued the American — had fallen in love too. Tante Estelle's anger was probably as much about jealousy as sisterly

152

betrayal. Oh, she could be wrong. But she didn't think so.

CHAPTER 12

On Saturday morning, Simone went down to the lobby for breakfast but was surprised to find Kyle down there, having coffee with Noel. "Just the girl I was hoping to see," Kyle called to Simone as she filled a coffee cup.

"And why is that?" She came over to greet them both.

"Because I hope you'll spend the day with me." He smiled warmly.

"I'd love to." She sipped her coffee. "What did you have in mind?"

"Well, Tante Estelle has given me the loan of her old car, and I'd like to do some exploring." He chuckled. "I'll warn you, it's a very old car. She wasn't even sure it would start, but I tinkered with it a bit, and now it's running just fine."

"So you're a clockmaker *and* a mechanic?"

"Let's just say I'm handy." He winked. "Now finish up that brew and we'll be on our way."

Noel told them to have a good day then turned to Kyle. "I will keep in mind what you said. Thank you."

Although Simone was curious about what Kyle had told Noel, she got the impression it was a private conversation. When Noel went to check on some other guests, Kyle told her he had some exciting news.

"Exciting news?" She set down her empty cup.

"Go get your coat and maybe some warmer clothes. I'll explain about the news in the car. I left it running to make sure it doesn't die."

As she hurried up to her room, she grew even more curious about Kyle's exciting news. She knew he'd spent a long day at the clock and watch factory yesterday. And then he'd had dinner plans afterward. Plans that hadn't included her. Not that she'd been particularly concerned . . . although she had felt a little worried that Sylvie had something to do with those plans. As she grabbed her scarf and gloves, she wondered if Sylvie might have offered him a full-time job at the factory. And, really, was it any of Simone's business? Except that she was suspicious of Sylvie's motives. She remembered Leon's warning that their cousin was unpredictable, that she ran hot and cold.

Outside the inn, Kyle was standing next to a charming old blue car. Its rounded shape reminded her of a Volkswagen Bug, except bigger. "What is it?" she asked him as he opened the passenger door.

"A 1948 Renault. And in mint condition too."

"It's really cute."

"It was your aunt's first and only car," he said as he got behind the wheel. "She got it to drive to the clock factory after her skiing accident. She only drove it to work, so it has less than sixty thousand miles on it. After she quit going to work, about twenty years ago, she's mostly kept it in the carriage house, although she used to drive it a bit in the summertime."

"Well, that was really generous of her to let you use it."

"I'll say. Of course, it was Sylvie's idea. And since I'll mostly use it to get to and from the clock factory, Tante Estelle agreed. I'm only taking it out today to make sure the battery is good and charged."

"Thus our winter wonderland drive."

"Exactly." He grinned.

"So is that your good news? That you get to use this car? Or is there something more?" She was still stuck on the fact that

Sylvie was behind the car loan idea. Did that mean Kyle was becoming a solid fixture in the family business?

"At dinner last night, Tante Estelle told us about your visit with her yesterday."

"Uh-huh?"

"And she actually mentioned your letter from your great-grandmother . . . about the treasure."

"She did?" Simone was surprised.

"Yes. She felt badly for the way she shut you down when you told her about it the other day. She wants to make it up to you."

"How's that?"

"Even though she doubts there really is a treasure, she's willing to let you look for it in her house . . . or wherever."

"Really? I can go poking around? With her blessing?"

"Well, blessing might be a stretch. To be fair, it was actually Sylvie's idea."

"Sylvie?"

"Yeah. Sylvie convinced her that it was the best way to wrap all this business up with you. Let you have your search and be done with it."

"So Sylvie doesn't believe there's a treasure either?"

He shrugged. "I'm not sure. At first, she seemed pretty dismissive about the whole thing. But then she got kind of interested. She even asked Tante Estelle what she'd do if you really did find a treasure in her house. She questioned whether it was fair for you to actually keep it. She thinks it should belong to the whole family."

"But if it really did belong to my great-grandmamma — and I have her letter saying she wants me to have it — wouldn't I be legally entitled to it?"

"Good question. But I'm clueless to French inheritance laws."

By now they were outside of town and, instead of continuing what had turned into a frustrating conversation, Simone commented on the enchanting farms and chalets. "This really is a beautiful part of France. I bet it's gorgeous in the springtime."

"I'm hoping I'll get to see that."

"Oh?" She glanced at him. "Are you planning to remain here — indefinitely?"

"I don't know about indefinitely. But I'd love to stay on for, say, six months or so. If they let me."

"Why wouldn't they let you?"

"Well, Sylvie only agreed to a monthlong apprenticeship. And after that, she said they can't afford to hire me. Of course, I'd probably work for free . . . for a while anyway.

Not that I told her."

"Why can't they afford to hire you?"

"Apparently, the factory is in the red. Steadily losing money. The watch factory name isn't big enough to bring in the market, despite the fact that their quality is similar to a Rolex. Besides that, people aren't buying old-fashioned clocks these days. At least, that's Sylvie's take on it. She wants to turn the company into something else — something more profitable. She mentioned a cosmetics factory." He glumly shook his head.

"That would be a shame. It's such a lovely old clock and watch factory." She remembered the old man who'd been painting the clockface and how his wife wanted him to retire. Maybe the clock business, like the old man, had become obsolete.

"Yeah," said Kyle, "I hate the idea of it disappearing."

"I wonder what Tante Estelle thinks about that. You know, she's the one who saved it from being shut down after the war. Isn't she the owner?"

"I heard she owns more than fifty percent of the company, but her family members all have a piece of the pie too. According to Sylvie, it's just a matter of time. When Tante Estelle passes, her share of the company will

159

be split among the relatives, then they can make changes as they like."

"That just makes me sad."

"Sorry, I wasn't trying to depress you." He stopped at a crossing. "Now what about searching through Tante Estelle's house? I thought maybe I could help you today."

She brightened. "That could be fun. Well, unless we actually found something and Sylvie decided I couldn't keep it."

"Seems like it would be up to Tante Estelle to make that call."

"Maybe, but I get the feeling Sylvie has a lot of influence over her. Certainly much more than I would have."

"Well, Sylvie's had a lot more time to get on your aunt's good side. Still, I got the distinct impression that Tante Estelle might warm up to you."

"Really?" Simone felt doubtful.

"I think it's possible. She's really much nicer than you think."

"Maybe to you since you seem to have the inside track." She didn't want to mention Sylvie again.

"Well, it probably helps that my French is a bit more polished than yours."

"I'm working on it. Anyway, I'm not surprised you've won my aunt over." Simone chuckled. "You seem rather adept at charm-

160

ing Beaumont women."

He laughed. "I'm not so sure about that. But I did make serious progress with her last night at dinner. Sylvie mentioned how I learned my clockmaking skills from my old neighbor. When I mentioned his name, your aunt grew very animated. Can you believe it, Claude Aron used to work at the Avre Clock and Watch Factory."

"Seriously? Did you know this before you came?"

Kyle shook his head. "I knew he lived in the French Alps, but I never knew the name of the town or the company."

"That's so amazing. I mean we meet on the plane and end up here and — well, it's just sort of mind-blowing."

"Almost seems preordained."

"So Tante Estelle knew your old friend Claude?" Simone asked.

"He was a few years ahead of her in school. Probably more your great-grandmother's age. But your aunt admired him, and she knew he worked at the clock and watch factory. Possibly the reason she became interested."

"And perhaps one more reason she is so drawn to you and welcoming you into her fold." Simone felt a pang of jealousy. Kyle was making much more progress with her family than she was.

"I think she'll welcome you too, Simone. Just give her time. This morning I mentioned I planned to see you today. She seems very curious about our relationship."

Simone's interest piqued. "I wonder why."

"I don't know. It might have to do with Sylvie." He frowned. "But anyway, I said I was going to let you know that she was okay with letting you search for your treasure. And her reaction was interesting."

"How's that?"

"Well, I could've imagined it, but she almost seemed amused."

"That's encouraging." Simone's spirits lifted. "So do you think the car battery is charged enough? Is it too soon to go back?"

He laughed. "Aha, so you're ready to go treasure hunting now?"

"Yes. Time's a-wasting." Suddenly she couldn't wait to start poking around. "Just last night, I was ruminating on Tante Estelle's story from yesterday — about how she and my great-grandmamma hid their American. First in the cellar and later in the attic. I got to thinking my great-grandmamma could have stashed something in either of those places. They seem better hiding spots than her bedroom. Don't you think?"

"Absolutely." As he turned the car around, he pointed to a dark cloud coming down from the mountains. "Looks like we've got more weather on the way. Good time to get back to town."

Simone didn't know what to expect when she and Kyle told Tante Estelle they were there to do some treasure hunting, but to her pleasant surprise, her unpredictable aunt seemed just fine. In fact, she even apologized to Simone for insisting there was no treasure the first time they'd met. Now she simply shrugged, admitting that perhaps there was a treasure. Who knew? Surely, Simone Sophia would not write about a treasure if none existed. Tante Estelle actually smiled, telling Simone to look to her heart's content.

Relieved to have what really did seem like her blessing, Simone and Kyle began their search in the cellar. This dark, damp place was a cross between seriously creepy and strangely intriguing. Old furnishings in need of repair, musty moth-chewed carpets, boxes of old clothes, children's toys, and much more. Much of it would probably be welcomed in a Los Angeles antique store or flea market, but here in France? Simone wasn't so sure. And she certainly didn't have a house to put any of it in.

"I wonder how long this has been the family home." Simone muttered as she placed a stack of cobweb-covered baskets back on the grimy wooden shelf. All of which, other than layers of dust, were empty.

"Tante Estelle told me her father was born in this house, and that it was built by his parents back in the late 1800s."

"So it's always been the Beaumont house." She sighed. "It must be cool to have that kind of heritage."

"It's your heritage too."

"Maybe, but I didn't grow up with it."

"You didn't grow up here in France, but you mentioned your grandparents raised you. That's a heritage too. But I don't remember why they raised you." He tugged on a box he'd just unearthed beneath a pile of old carpets.

"Probably because I didn't say." She still hadn't told him everything about her mother's abandonment. Maybe someday.

"Hey, look at this." He dragged the heavy box away from the wall, carefully setting it upright.

Simone went closer, studying the old wooden box. With the tarnished brass latch, it seemed to have real treasure chest potential. She knelt down to try the latch but couldn't get it to budge. "Do you think this could be it? *The treasure?*"

"Ready for the drumroll?" He went over to a tool bench, returning with a blackened screwdriver. "Want me to open it?"

"Of course!" She watched with wide eyes as he carefully pried the latch open, then stepped back, waiting for Simone to lift the lid. "It's just wine." She removed a bottle from a nest of old straw then studied the yellow label. "Bordeaux 1923. Think it's any good?"

"I don't know, but I'll bet it's pretty valuable."

"How much do you think it's worth?"

"Could be upwards of three hundred dollars a bottle. Maybe more."

"And all the bottles seem to be full." She paused to do the math. "This whole case could be worth $3,600!"

"The treasure hunt pays off." He examined the bottle more closely. "We can look up the value online. If it's an important vineyard, you never know. I've heard of old bottles going for in the thousands."

"Wow." She carefully slid the bottle back in.

"Do you think this is the treasure your great-grandmother meant?"

"I doubt it. First of all, she was only

eighteen when she left. And I doubt this wine would've been worth so much back then, so she probably wouldn't have considered it to be a treasure. But we should take it up for Tante Estelle to see." She glanced around the dimly lit cellar. "In fact, there are a lot of things down here that could have value. If the clock and watch factory is in as bad of financial shape as Sylvie says, it seems some of this stuff could be sold and invested in the company."

Kyle picked up the heavy box. "Lead the way. We'll show Tante Estelle that your treasure hunt is beneficial to her too."

They found her in the library, reading the newspaper. Kyle announced that they'd found a "little treasure." Tante Estelle's brows arched slightly as Kyle set the crate on the floor then removed a bottle.

"Tell her it could be very valuable," Simone urged him. "And tell her there are other antiques and collectibles down there that could be sold as well. And that I'm happy to go through everything for her. I can sort and clean and get it ready to sell. Then she could use the proceeds to help the clock factory."

Kyle explained all this and, although Tante Estelle seemed slightly amused, she dismissively waved her hand before she responded.

Kyle looked disappointed as he relayed it to Simone. "She says thank you for your kind offer, but there's no need for you to go to so much trouble for her." He let out what sounded like a discouraged sigh. "It seems this house and everything in it has already been mortgaged to the bank. For the sake of the clock and watch factory. She said she made this arrangement about ten years ago in order to keep her company from going bankrupt. The agreement with the mortgage company is that she can remain in her home for the rest of her days. And I think she assumes the factory will remain intact as a result."

"So she doesn't realize her company might not survive . . . after she's gone?" Simone asked quietly. "She's not aware of its current financial troubles?"

"I guess not. Do you think I should tell her?"

Simone bit her lip. "I don't know. I mean, there's not much she can do about it. Especially if she's already mortgaged everything of value here. Still, this is sad."

"I know." Kyle made a forced-looking smile for Tante Estelle's sake. "Maybe ignorance really is bliss." He held out the bottle of wine now, asking what she wanted done with it.

"Ouvrez la bouteille," she declared brightly. "Seriously?" Simone was shocked. "She wants to *open* it? Doesn't she understand it could be very valuable?"

Kyle explained this, but Tante Estelle simply lifted her hand, as if holding a glass to make a toast, demanding again that he open the bottle. And with her gray eyes glittering with excitement, she eagerly gave Kyle more instructions.

"She asked me to take it to Willa for decanting," Kyle told Simone. "She wants it served with a late lunch, in the parlor, with us as her guests."

"Do you think it's safe to drink such old wine?" Simone quietly asked Kyle.

"Sure. But chances are it'll taste like vinegar and no one will want to drink it."

"Okay then . . ." Simone looked down at her dirty hands. "Guess I should clean up a bit." So far her treasure hunt hadn't exactly produced anything . . . well, other than a bit of fun and the promise of lunch with a bottle of wine that would probably taste like vinegar. Maybe that was enough.

CHAPTER 13

While Kyle took the wine to the kitchen, Simone went to wash up. It felt good to roam freely through this big old house with no worries her aunt might take after her with a raised cane. She found the powder room tucked under the staircase. It was neat and clean with pale pink fixtures and faded climbing-rose wallpaper. Obviously an upgrade from the late 1800s, but still vintage. Even the little linen guest towels with an embroidered *B* for Beaumont seemed to be from a time gone by.

Before long, the three of them were seated around the little round table in the parlor. On a lace tablecloth, china plates of meats and cheeses, fruits, and even slices of lovely bread, were prettily arranged. Centered on the table was a sparkling crystal decanter, with dark red wine. Estelle instructed Kyle to fill the crystal goblets and, after swirling hers and sniffing deeply, she smiled.

"Aromatique?" Kyle asked.

"Oui." She ceremonially lifted her goblet for a toast. "À votre santé."

Kyle and Simone echoed her toast to their health. But Simone, still a bit worried, waited for her elderly aunt to take the first sip. Then seeing Kyle bravely tasting his, Simone took a cautious sample, bracing herself for vinegar. To her surprise, it wasn't half bad.

"Très bon," Kyle declared.

"Oui!" Estelle eagerly nodded. "C'est très bon!"

"Bon," Simone agreed. Although she wasn't a true wine aficionado, she was relieved it didn't taste bitter. And suddenly, getting caught up in the spirit, she was moved at the idea of sharing a nearly hundred-year-old wine with her great-great-aunt and good friend Kyle. It felt like a memorable moment.

As the three of them enjoyed their late leisurely lunch, Kyle inquired about the clock and watch factory's history. Simone, eager to hear this story, begged her aunt to speak slowly to help her understand without too much translation help. Tante Estelle seemed to respect this, taking her time to tell her tale, starting with the onset of World War II.

Estelle had been a carefree young girl when Hitler began rising to power. Her family was not wealthy, but comfortable. Although many friends and neighbors fled France due to bad memories of the previous war, her family remained in Avre where their father had a prominent legal practice. Her two older brothers, Jean and Basile, left to serve with the French Army. And Simone Sophia went to work in the clock and watch factory. The factory was busy providing military watches and items for military use.

Kyle asked which side the company made the watches for, and Tante Estelle told him *both* the Allied Forces and the Germans. Then with a sly expression, she admitted that much less care went into the watches for the Nazis. Her eyes grew sad as she relayed how Basile was killed in battle, leaving behind not only her family but also a young wife and infant son. About a year later, Jean died in a German prison camp. And then Simone Sophia left with the American. Their family had shrunk to three. Her papa, little brother, and Estelle.

She was only seventeen when she went to work at the clock and watch factory, but she loved the work and her coworkers helped make up for the losses in her family. After the war ended, Estelle continued at the factory, but the economy was weak and after a few years of struggles, the clock and watch factory was going to shut down. Although she was only twenty-one, Estelle made arrangements to purchase the company. She did so discreetly and with her father's legal guidance, since some people wouldn't approve of a young woman running a company that mostly employed men.

At this point in the story, Simone asked her aunt if she'd ever considered marriage. Tante Estelle took in a deep breath then answered by simply saying the war took the best men, so she preferred to remain single and enjoy her independence. Besides, she was married to the clock and watch factory. With her modernizations and the improving economy, business picked up. Estelle lived happily and comfortably. Doing as she pleased . . . until her skiing accident. But even with a crippled hip, she still enjoyed her work at the factory.

It wasn't long before the company became prosperous and life seemed to be looking up. But then her papa passed away with a heart attack. Arnou was in college and Estelle was able to cover his tuition until graduation when he joined the clock and watch factory. The company continued to thrive and grow. Certainly, they had some hard times when the economy dipped, but somehow they were always able to recover. All and all, she was very pleased to leave such a successful company behind. The clock and watch factory was her legacy for the town of Avre. She leaned back in her chair, sighing happily.

Simone exchanged glances with Kyle but said nothing. Instead, she smiled at her aunt, congratulating her for all that she'd accomplished in life. What did it hurt if she didn't know the real fate of her beloved company? And it was true that she was leaving *something* behind. Sure, it might morph into a cosmetics company, but it still had value and would employ locals.

Kyle and Simone thanked Tante Estelle for the delightful lunch and, for the rest of the day, searched through the attic. Although they found a number of interesting "treasures," they never unearthed anything that seemed the sort of thing a young woman might leave behind. Simone was more convinced than ever that her great-grandmamma's treasure had simply been a figment of her well-aged imagination.

When Tante Estelle insisted they share an early dinner with her, they didn't argue. Tired and dusty, they sat and listened while she continued to reminisce over times gone by. The stories were interesting, and she clearly enjoyed telling them. Plus, Simone's French was improving because she seemed to need less help with translation. At least, when the old woman spoke slowly.

As they got ready to leave, Tante Estelle expressed her sympathy that their search was unfruitful, but she didn't seem surprised. As they put on their coats, she offered Simone a few more search tips. She suggested a few places where Simone Sophia had frequented. Perhaps she'd stashed something away where no one ever found it. It was possible, no?

Simone thanked her, but as they cleaned freshly fallen snow from the old car, she had her doubts. She felt fairly certain she'd come to France on a wild-goose chase. Although it'd been fun — especially with Kyle's help — was it worthwhile to keep pursuing what felt increasingly senseless?

"Are you discouraged?" Kyle asked as he drove her home.

"A little. I mean, it would've been fun to find something my great-grandmamma had left behind. But I'm wondering . . . seriously, what kind of treasure could she have possibly had when she was only eighteen years old?"

"Good question. Even though she worked

at the factory and even if she'd saved every cent, it couldn't have amounted to much."

"My thinking exactly. Plus, Tante Estelle said they weren't a wealthy family."

"I am curious as to how she interprets *wealthy,*" Kyle said. "Compared to how I grew up — I mean, based on all those fine antique pieces of furniture, fancy china, silver and crystal, original art pieces . . . not to mention the old stuff we've seen in her cellar and attic. Well, that family seemed to be pretty well off. At least to me."

"I had similar thoughts. Although it seems the bank owns everything now anyway. But even if her family had been wealthy at one time, my great-grandmamma sort of ran away, so I doubt they would've given her anything of value. Plus, it was wartime. All the belts were tightened. I honestly don't get it."

"Well, other than going through Tante Estelle's room, it seems like we pretty much cased the entire house today." Kyle glanced her way. "Can you think of anything we missed?"

"No, but I'm curious about her suggestion to search the clock factory. And the family church. Even the family's favorite ski resort. Doesn't that seem a little far-fetched to think anything could be hidden in those places?"

"I don't know, but I wouldn't mind going to church tomorrow anyway. Care to join me? Who knows? We might discover some sort of clue there. At the very least, we might get some spiritual encouragement."

She nodded. "Sure, that sounds great."

"And if Tante Estelle lends me a key, we could poke around the factory in the afternoon. Might be easier on a Sunday when no one's around to question us, though, to be honest, it will probably be like searching for a needle in a haystack."

"I know." Simone sighed. "But it might be fun."

He grinned. "Then it's a date."

Church was surprisingly enjoyable. The ancient building was gorgeous with enormous stained glass windows and ornately carved wood. It was decorated for Christmas with evergreens, red roses, and white satin ribbons. Plus, something about hymns and Christmas songs sung in French was deeply moving to Simone. She knew her great-grandmamma had always loved attending church, and it was touching to think this was the very same church she'd been baptized in as a girl. Still, there was nothing to lead either Kyle or Simone to believe she'd hidden something of value here. Well, besides memories.

Their next stop was the clock and watch factory. Kyle unlocked the door and turned on the lights. "Tante Estelle must really trust you," Simone said as they went inside, "to give you her key."

"I think she trusts you even more." He closed and relocked the door. "You are, after all, her great-great-niece."

"Do you think she really trusts me?"

He nodded as he turned on more lights. "Just this morning, she said some very complimentary things about you."

"What?" she asked eagerly.

"I don't know if I should repeat them. There might be a reason she never says such things while you're around."

"And what would that be?"

He chuckled. "She might be worried you'll get a big head."

"Oh, please." She rolled her eyes.

"Yes, I doubt you'd let her words go to your head." He peered closely at her. "Well, for starters, your aunt thinks you are very beautiful. Perhaps even more so than her older sister was as a girl. But besides that, she believes you have a *true spirit*. That's how she described it. And she believes you are genuinely good and kind."

"Wow, that's really sweet. She honestly said all that?"

"That and more. I can tell she is really glad that she's been able to get to know you. She said it helps to make up for the heartbreak of losing her sister." He led her into a storage room. "I think this could be a good place to poke around. Lots of really old stuff in here."

"What you said about making up for losing her sister" — Simone opened a tall cupboard, staring blankly at boxes of items she couldn't even identify — "I'm still puzzled over why there was such a rift between them. For so many years. My great-grandmamma never even spoke of a sister. And when I first met Tante Estelle, well, you heard how that went."

"Yes, but she's really warmed up to you. Maybe it was just that the family was hurt when Simone Sophia ran off with your great-grandfather." He opened a drawer, studying the contents with interest. "They probably felt abandoned. And then she went through such hard times . . . the war, losing two brothers, then her father."

"Yeah, that makes sense. Plenty of room for resentment."

"Wow, I can't believe how well stocked they are with some really old stuff." He held up a small box of watch parts as if to prove his point. "If I ran this company, I'd start manufacturing retro-vintage watches with the original pieces."

"Not a bad idea."

"It makes me wonder if Sylvie is giving up too easily on this business." He closed the large drawer then opened another.

"Well, you said she doesn't even like the business. It's not surprising she wants to give up on it. From what I can tell from Oncle Arnou, Emile is not a businessman."

"I agree. I already observed that Sylvie's dad cares more about clockmaking than management. And he's very good at it. He seemed convinced that Sylvie's business degree would be the answer for the factory's problems. There's no denying that woman has a business head."

The more they searched, the more they both felt it was useless. "Honestly, even if there was a treasure hidden here somewhere, I doubt we could ever find it." Kyle paused by a clockmaker's station, examining what looked like a work in progress. "It's so depressing to think this company will be kaput after Tante Estelle passes away. And she won't last forever."

"I know." Simone studied the painting on a clockface. "This looks fun, Kyle. I wish I could give it a try."

He came over to look. "You have an artistic streak?"

She shrugged. "Before I became a dental assistant, I was very interested in art."

"You know, I've heard that dentists have a similar set of skills to clock and watchmakers. If you're good with your hands as well as creative, you could be a valuable asset here." He chuckled. "Not that they're hiring."

"What if I worked for free? Just to give it a try. Do you think Sylvie would let me?"

"I think Tante Estelle would let you," he said.

"Then I'm going to ask her," Simone declared. "With nearly a whole week until Christmas, I'd love to have something to occupy myself with. Something besides searching for some nonexistent treasure."

"Meaning you're giving up?"

"Not completely. But maybe taking a break."

It was all arranged by Monday morning. Thanks to Tante Estelle, Simone would have a mini apprenticeship with Pierre, the elderly artist she'd spoken with last week. Pierre couldn't have been happier. Sylvie not so much. But the work was fun, and it didn't take long before Pierre entrusted Simone with her own clockface, assuring her it could always be painted over if she messed it up. But by the end of the day, when she managed to get it just right, Pierre was ecstatic. He carried the face around for others to admire, telling everyone what a good teacher he'd been.

"When do you return to America?" Sylvie asked Simone as she pulled on her coat to go home. "I heard you remain here through Christmas. My grandpapa says you are to join *our* family festivities, no?"

"Yes. That's right." Simone wrapped her scarf around her neck. Sylvie's tone made it clear she didn't want her American cousin horning in on *her* family. But weren't they Simone's family too?

"Ready to call it quits after a hard day's work?" Kyle asked Simone.

"A hard day's fun is more like it." She smiled at him. "Yes, ready."

He turned to Sylvie. "You're still coming to Noel's surprise birthday party tomorrow night?"

"Oui." She brightened. "You will pick me up?"

"Sure," he agreed. "Noel will be pleased to have you there."

"And you? You will be pleased too?" Her

eyes sparkled with blatant flirtation.

"Of course." He turned back to Simone. "Ready?"

As they went out to the car, Simone felt another jab of jealousy. Sylvie obviously had more than a casual interest in Kyle. But did he feel the same — or was he just being polite? Whatever the case, she didn't intend to ask. Maybe she didn't want to know. Instead, she chattered away about how much she'd enjoyed working with Pierre today and how he really was a good teacher and how she thought she could do work like that for years and years and never grow tired of it.

"So much better than working in a dental clinic, putting your hands in strangers' mouths." She shuddered to remember how much she'd hated that job. Kyle asked how she'd gotten into that line of work, and she explained about her practical grandmother. "I sort of let her talk me into it," she said.

"My parents wanted me to be a CPA," Kyle admitted. "That's because they had their own accounting firm and thought I should step into it."

"Not for you?"

"Nah. I was hooked on computers by middle school. My buddy and I were sort of geeks. Always working on something. I only finished two years of college before we started our own company. My parents were shocked at how well that turned out for me, although my mom still doesn't understand why I sold my half of the company. But she did like the idea of me coming over here. She plans to sell the firm this spring. Then she wants to retire and do some traveling in Europe. Hopefully while I'm still over here."

"That would be nice for her. Do you think you'll stay in Avre that long?"

"I don't know for sure." As he pulled up to the inn, Kyle slapped his forehead. "I nearly forgot. Tante Estelle wants you to come stay at her house."

"Really?"

"Yes. She feels guilty that you're at the inn and asked me to insist you change accommodations. She wants you to stay with her through Christmas."

"That's so sweet of her. I'd like to do it, but how about I make the switch tomorrow — after work?"

"Great. I'll let her know as soon as I get home. I told her I'll gladly vacate the guest room so you can have a better —"

"No, no, please, I'd rather be in my great-grandmamma's old room. That would feel really special to me. You keep the guest room."

"Pretty dusty in that room."

"That's okay. Let Tante Estelle know I'm happy to clean it myself. I don't want to be any trouble for her or Willa. Especially so close to the holidays."

"Okay. See you in the morning."

As Simone went inside, she had mixed feelings. On one hand she was honored that Tante Estelle was welcoming her into her home. On the other hand, the comfortable inn had come to feel like home. Even so, she paused at the main desk to let Noel's mother know about her change of plans.

"What? Is something wrong?" Marie frowned.

"No, no." Simone explained how much she loved the inn and how warm and cozy it was, but that her aunt wanted her to stay with her. Marie smiled, agreeing it was best to be with family for Christmas. Then she quietly asked if Simone would still attend Noel's birthday celebration.

"Oui!" Simone eagerly nodded, assuring Marie she was looking forward to it. And she was mostly looking forward to it . . . except for the Sylvie factor. Simone knew that Sylvie was determined to win over Kyle.

CHAPTER 14

On Simone's second day at the clock and watch factory, she already felt like she belonged. The other employees seemed glad to have her there and even put up with her language challenges. They clearly enjoyed their work, and their camaraderie was obvious. And since it was their last workday until after Christmas, people had brought treats, which put everyone in an extra jovial mood. She could easily imagine how Tante Estelle had found a sense of family with her co-workers. The only fly in the ointment was Sylvie. She clearly didn't enjoy Simone's presence in the factory . . . or even in the country, for that matter.

At the end of the day, everyone was sharing Christmas greetings and getting ready to leave. As Simone slipped into her coat, she could see Sylvie openly flirting with Kyle — again. Reminding him to pick her up, she playfully teased about the evening ahead, even describing the low-cut dress she planned to wear. The shameless woman even fluttered her eyelashes. Well, unless Simone imagined it — and that was possible.

Still, Simone would never tell a guy — even one she was very fond of — about what she planned to wear on a date. Perhaps that was a French thing. The fact was, Simone didn't know what she would wear tonight, but hearing about Sylvie's wardrobe plans, she knew she would probably step it up. At least she knew that was what Andrea would advise.

She'd only spoken to Andrea once since arriving in Avre, and so, while Kyle exchanged greetings, Simone stepped outside and pulled out her phone. To her disappointment the call went straight to voicemail. As she walked over to Kyle's car, she left a quick message for Andrea then waited for Kyle next to his borrowed car.

Kyle had already loaded her luggage in the Renault's trunk, which was oddly located in the front of the car. The plan was to go directly to Tante Estelle's after the workday ended. Simone still felt bad remembering how disappointed Noel had been when she checked out. He actually seemed close to tears — and on his birthday too! She felt so guilty that she'd almost blurted out something about seeing him this evening. Thankfully, she hadn't.

She shivered as an icy wind whipped past the clock factory building. It looked like new snow was headed this way. To her relief Kyle was just exiting, hurrying toward her to open up the car.

"Tante Estelle is so happy that you're moving in, she's planned a special dinner." Kyle said as he helped her inside.

"And she knows about our plans to go to the birthday party tonight?"

"I told her. She said Willa will make it an early dinner."

"Perfect."

"She also insisted Willa would clean and freshen your room for you."

"I hope it wasn't too much trouble." Simone had never gotten the feeling that Willa really liked her, but perhaps it was due to getting off on the wrong foot . . . or crashing tea parties. Hopefully their relationship would improve now.

At Tante Estelle's, Simone found her bedroom completely cleaned out. Not only had Willa put in fresh linens and a newer bedspread, there was also a small vase of pink rosebuds on the dresser. She felt very welcomed.

The table in the formal dining room was elegantly set with china, crystal, silver, candlesticks, and more rosebuds. Once again there was a decanter of dark red wine, and Tante Estelle explained it was from the crate they'd found in the cellar, toasting this time to family. The food and conversation were so lovely at the dinner table that Simone almost didn't want to excuse themselves for the birthday party. Except she knew Noel would be disappointed.

"I forgot to tell you how pretty you look," Kyle said after they were in the car.

"Thank you." She felt her cheeks warming. "Looks like we're in for more snow."

Kyle nodded. "I hear the skiing is excellent."

"Tante Estelle asked me if we'd gone up to their favorite ski resort yet."

"That's right. She suggested it was a place for our treasure hunt." He laughed. "I actually think she's just leading us on now."

"Hey, I have an idea! What if we invited her to go to the lodge with us? She used to love skiing. I'll bet she hasn't been up there in ages."

"I love that idea. The factory is closed until after Christmas, so maybe we could drive up there tomorrow."

"I wonder if we could talk her into it."

"We'll find out." They drove for a little while before Kyle parked in front of a modern-looking apartment building that really didn't seem to fit in with the town. "This is where Sylvie lives. Do you think I should be a gentleman and go to her door or just text her to come down?"

Simone shrugged, suddenly uneasy. "I, uh, I don't know. Is this supposed to be a date for you two? Should I get in the back seat?"

"No, of course not. It's definitely not a date. Not with Sylvie anyway." He grinned at Simone. "I wouldn't mind if it was a date with you."

A wave of relief washed over her. "Really?"

"Absolutely."

"So you're not interested in Sylvie?" she asked shyly.

"Only as my boss."

"Well, have you noticed that she is quite interested in you?"

He laughed. "Hard not to."

"It's probably flattering." She tried to repress feelings of jealousy.

"Like it's flattering when Noel pays that same kind of attention to you?"

She blinked. "You noticed that?"

"Of course. And it made me pretty jealous too." He chuckled. "So jealous that I've been trying to play cupid between Noel and Sylvie."

"Seriously?"

He nodded with a sheepish grin. "I told Noel that I thought Sylvie might be interested in him. Then I said the same thing to her. That's why I insisted she should come tonight." His laugh deepened. "I hoped that if those two were distracted with each other, I would have you all to myself."

She giggled. "I had no idea you were such a schemer."

He leaned closer to her. "You have *no* idea." And, just like that, he kissed her. "I hope that was okay." He moved back with an uneasy smile.

"It was more than okay." She smiled back. "But what about Sylvie?"

"I'll text her."

Having Sylvie ride in the back seat on the way to the inn turned out to be just the thing to communicate Kyle's level of interest. Unfortunately, her nose was seriously out of joint as they walked into the birthday party. But since it was almost time for Noel to arrive and everyone had to lie low while Marie turned off the lights, Sylvie never had the chance to vocalize her complaints. Kyle led Simone to a spot near the reception desk, holding her hand in the darkened room where only the Christmas tree lights were visible.

Marie whispered that Noel was at the door, and the room grew silent. Noel came into the strangely darkened lobby, and as Marie turned the lights back on, everyone yelled "Surprise!" Poor Noel was so shocked that he literally fell down in front of the reception desk, and Marie and Kyle rushed over to help him to his feet.

As he stood, he started laughing hysterically, and then everyone else began to laugh — and to greet him, wishing him a happy birthday. Simone sneaked a peek at Sylvie, who was sitting alone by the fireplace with a glowering expression. Hopefully her disillusionment over Kyle wouldn't put a damper on the party for Noel. Simone considered making an attempt to cheer her cousin but suspected that might be like throwing gas on a fire.

As jazz music began to play, a few couples started to dance. And before long, Simone was actually dancing with Kyle. Sure, neither of them were great dancers, but it was still fun. Then after a while, and much to Simone's great relief, Noel and Sylvie were dancing too. And they were excellent dancers!

"I think your attempt at playing cupid was successful," she whispered to Kyle as they danced to a slow song.

"Good!" He pulled her even closer, sending a happy shiver through her.

By the time the party ended, Sylvie seemed to have completely forgotten Kyle. And when he announced that he and Simone were leaving, she informed him she no longer needed a ride — Noel would take her home!

"That was a lovely party," she said as Kyle drove them down the snowy streets. "I can't remember ever having a better time."

"I was just thinking the same thing."

"I know it's partly from being in France — the French certainly know how to live," she continued. "But it was also from being with you."

He reached over to grasp her hand, giving it a warm squeeze. "It was pretty magical."

As he drove through the snowy little town, she had to agree. Tonight was totally magical. And the idea of spending Christmas with Kyle and her French family members felt magical too. She only felt a small tinge of regret . . . she'd never found Great-grandmamma's treasure. Or perhaps there never was one. Maybe it didn't matter.

Estelle had been thrilled at the idea of seeing her favorite ski resort again. When it was time to go, following breakfast the next morning, she emerged from her bedroom dressed in a blue-and-white Nordic ski sweater, black stretch pants, and fur-trimmed boots. Simone complimented her, saying she looked very sporty. This made Estelle laugh. She showed them a moth hole in her sweater sleeve cuff, then confessed how these old clothes made her feel young again.

Still, she went slowly with her cane as they walked outside on the snow-covered footpath. Kyle stayed close by, supporting her free arm before he carefully helped her into the front seat of the car. Naturally, their plan wasn't to actually ski but to simply visit the lodge, look around a bit, and perhaps watch the skiers for a while. At least for as long as Tante Estelle felt like staying.

Last night, when Kyle had kissed Simone good night at the landing on the stairs, he had promised that the two of them would go up to the ski resort sometime after Christmas, and although he wasn't a great skier, he would do his best to help her give it a try. But for today, they would just be spectators.

Kyle and Estelle chatted congenially back and forth in front, but because of the car noise and her aunt's excited speech, Simone could barely make out their words. She decided to simply relax, watch the wintry landscape along the road, and daydream . . . mostly about her and Kyle. She had no doubts about his feelings for her now. Oh, no one had used the word *love* yet. Just the same, she felt fairly certain she was falling in love with him. To be honest, she'd probably fallen for him two weeks ago on the flight to Iceland. She only hoped he felt the same . . . or nearly.

The ski resort was charming and picturesque. Definitely from a bygone era with its quaint wooden structures and shuttered windows. Tante Estelle told them it was built in the early 1900s and that her parents used to love to come here. They came here for their honeymoon and later on brought the children up for a few unforgettable Christmases. As she reminisced about her early childhood — before losing her mother — her eyes lit up as if the young girl were still inside.

They finally settled in the main lodge, in front of a big stone fireplace. Kyle brought them hot drinks, crafted to Estelle's specification. And with her attentive audience, she continued to chatter about childhood memories. She claimed to be the best skier of the five children. Even her father used to brag about how she'd fearlessly attack the slopes, proving to be even braver than her two older brothers.

Kyle was such an attentive audience that Simone knew she wouldn't be missed if she excused herself to explore the lodge a bit more. Exchanging glances with Kyle, she suspected he'd already guessed her real intent — to poke around a bit . . . just in case there was some hidden treasure here. But the more she looked, the more she knew it was in vain. Why would her great-grandmamma hide something valuable in a public place like this?

Although still clearly enjoying herself, Tante Estelle looked weary when Simone rejoined them. She asked her aunt if it was time to go, but Tante Estelle instantly rallied, declaring they should first have lunch.

Because it was a bit early still, they were able to get a table by the window. Tante Estelle insisted they all try what had been her family's favorite dish up here — raclette! A cheesy dish with Gruyère cheese, potatoes, onions, pickles, and dried meats — it was delicious! All in all, it was a delightful visit to the nearby ski resort, and Simone looked forward to going there again — just her and Kyle!

CHAPTER 15

Back at the house, Estelle admitted she was bone weary and in need of a nice long nap. Still smiling over their unexpected winter excursion, she solemnly proclaimed that she could now die happy. Simone exchanged glances with Kyle as Estelle tottered off to her bedroom. "Hopefully she didn't mean that literally," Simone said quietly as she removed her parka. "I've barely gotten to know her. I'd be devastated if she died now."

"Don't worry. That old gal still has a lot of life left in her. Couldn't you see that today?"

"She did seem younger. I wasn't sure if it was her sporty outfit or her joy at being at the resort, but she was definitely energetic." Simone put her coat away then opened the door to the library, glancing longingly at the darkened fireplace. "Do you suppose this fireplace works?"

"You bet it does. My first night here, Tante

Estelle had me make her a fire." He pulled his jacket back on. "There's a stack of wood next to the carriage house. I'll go get some."

"And I'll make us a pot of tea."

"It's a deal."

It wasn't long before they were comfortably seated in the library, with a crackling fire snapping cheerfully and a steamy pot of Earl Grey tea. "This is cozy." Simone handed Kyle his cup. "And Christmassy too. Nothing like being in LA."

"Did Tante Estelle tell you about the Beaumont family Christmas traditions?"

"Not exactly. Oncle Arnou did mention festivities at his house."

"That's right. They usually spend Christmas Eve here at Tante Estelle's house and Christmas Day at Oncle Arnou's." He grinned. "I'm invited too."

"I'd be shocked if you weren't. They seemed to adopt you as family — more quickly than me."

"You know, Simone, I've been thinking about something." His tone grew more serious than usual, making her heart beat a little faster. Was this about them? Was he going to proclaim his love? Was she even ready for that?

"Uh-huh?" She tucked her feet under her on the sofa, waiting nervously.

"Well, I get sad every time I think about the clock and watch company going under . . . you know, when Tante Estelle passes."

"Oh." Simone nodded, partly disappointed, partly relieved, but mostly just curious. "I know what you mean. It makes me sad too. Even more sad now that I've spent a little time working there. All those sweet people losing their jobs — it's heartbreaking. What will they do?"

"I doubt they'll want to work in the cosmetics factory." He scowled.

"Not exactly a clockmaker's dream job."

"It really bothers me that Tante Estelle is clueless about it. It seems so wrong." Suddenly he began talking fast, pouring out an idea for investing his own funds, which were considerable, to keep the factory afloat.

"Seriously?" She leaned forward, blinking. "You'd really do that?"

"Well, I'd have to get some legal advice and make sure that I was protecting my assets. But, yeah, I'd gladly do that if it all worked out fairly for everyone. And I'd want to have some control in the direction of the company."

"Wow." Simone leaned back.

"Does that sound crazy?"

She was still ruminating on all this.

"My mom will probably think I've lost my mind. But I had planned to invest in something, and I love clockmaking. Am I nuts, Simone?" His hazel eyes looked intently at her. "Has Avre put me under its spell?"

"I don't think so. . . ." She took in a slow deep breath. "In fact, I would probably consider doing the exact same thing. I mean, if everything could be worked out fairly, like you said. It makes sense."

"What do you mean? You want to be an investor too?"

She told him about selling her grandma's house and how that money was just sitting in the bank. "But I really do love the clock and watch factory," she said slowly, her realization growing. "And I love this town. And most of all, I love Tante Estelle. I hate the idea of her company vanishing when she's gone. It just feels so wrong."

Kyle jumped out of the chair and, coming over to sit on the sofa next to Simone, took both her hands. "That's awesome! We could do this thing together. Should we tell Tante Estelle about our idea?"

"Why not?"

"What about Sylvie? Should we reveal her plan to change things? Explain what's really going on?"

"I'm not sure about that." Simone thought

of the ramifications. "Maybe that's too much."

"Just the same, we could see if Tante Estelle would be willing to let us become partners with her in order to save the factory."

"Absolutely." Simone nodded. "I have no idea how she'll respond, but I totally love this idea. It's exciting and fun — and oh, I really hope she wants to do this."

"We'll have to broach it carefully." Kyle rubbed his chin. "We don't want to offend or upset her."

"I choose you to be our spokesperson," she said. "For one thing, your French is superior to mine. Besides that, I know Tante Estelle appreciates your business sense and experience."

Kyle agreed. And after a light dinner, he asked Tante Estelle if they could have a little meeting in the library. There, with the fire still going, he gently explained their fears about the future of the clock and watch factory. Without mentioning Sylvie's plans to convert it to a cosmetics factory, he confided that her family had concerns. At first Estelle seemed shocked to hear they were in such dire straits. But then she nodded, as if she understood. She admitted it wasn't the first time the company had faced financial difficulties. But hopefully it would rebound again . . . in time. Then she sighed, held up her hands, and said she was far too old and too poor to resolve it anyway, but as she said this, her eyes grew misty. Her heart clearly ached to know her beloved company's future was in peril.

Simone and Kyle exchanged knowing glances, then Kyle jumped in to lay out their partnership idea. Estelle's frown suggested confusion, or perhaps she simply doubted the validity of their offer or their ability to fulfill it. She questioned them in a stern tone, demanding to know how they could possibly propose such an idea.

So Kyle got very specific about numbers, projections, expectations, and responsibilities. Clearly the son of two CPAs, not to mention an entrepreneur of his own company, he seemed to have it all figured out. Simone couldn't grasp all he was saying, but Tante Estelle listened with a very focused expression, eagerly nodding from time to time.

Finally, he assured her that they'd want it all drawn up legally, fairly, for everyone. He turned to Simone, inviting her to contribute. She explained that all she wanted was to see the company preserved, and for all the devoted employees to continue with their work. Possibly with a few improvements to make the work atmosphere better, including better lighting and heating. Her aunt agreed.

Now Kyle looked intently at Tante Estelle, plainly asking if she thought this wild plan was even possible. Her eyes lit up as she assured him it was very possible. Then he asked about her other family members — would they agree?

Speaking at a slower pace so Simone could comprehend, she explained that Arnou and Emile each had a twenty percent share of the company that she'd gifted them upon her retirement. But she had retained sixty percent. According to her last will and testament, her share was to be divided equally between her two nieces, Sylvie and her sister, and her one nephew, Leon — making everyone equal shareholders. But she had planned to add Simone to this inheritance to make it a four-way split.

Tante Estelle paused and, resting a crooked finger aside her wrinkled cheek, her brow furrowed as if doing arithmetic. But Simone was ahead of her, calculating the number of Sylvie's family members that she might try to influence. If Sylvie's father, grandfather, and sister sided with her cosmetics company idea, they would have a solid majority of seventy percent. Even Leon couldn't be counted on if he needed funds to invest in his café.

It was crystal clear that if Tante Estelle were no longer in the picture, Sylvie and her family could easily control the company. Any investments made by Kyle and Simone would be at serious risk. And so, despite her earlier resolve not to mention Sylvie's future plans, Simone told her aunt about the cosmetics factory idea, quickly adding that she should go directly to Sylvie to hear the real story.

Tante Estelle's eyes flashed as she grabbed her cane and, pounding it into the floor with a solid thud, declared that that would happen over her dead body! And then, as if realizing the irony of her statement, she smiled grimly but firmly nodded. She would accept Kyle and Simone's offer of financial and managerial help, but first she would make some changes to her will.

Tante Estelle assured them she would make an appointment with her attorney right after Christmas. He would draft an agreement that would protect the future of the clock and watch company as well as Kyle's and Simone's investments. Then she would schedule a family meeting to inform everyone of these changes. She felt certain her brother and nephew would welcome this new direction because they, like her, loved the factory. As for the younger generation. "C'est la vie!" she proclaimed.

She slowly stood, declaring that she intended to live long enough to see this fiscal crisis resolved and the factory solidly back on its feet again. Hopefully within the upcoming year. They all shook hands on this and Tante Estelle, admitting she was very, very tired, said a weary bonsoir.

Kyle and Simone bid her good night but remained in the library. They were both still slightly stunned over what they'd just verbally agreed to do but before long, were eagerly discussing the future of the company and what they wanted to do to make it profitable. Admittedly most of the manufacturing ideas and improvements were Kyle's, but Simone wholeheartedly supported them. And when she shared some thoughts on making the workplace more pleasant for employees, he agreed.

Simone let out a sleepy yawn as Kyle pointed to the mantle clock. "It's getting late and tomorrow is Christmas Eve — probably a busy day for everyone. Maybe we should call it a night."

"I think you're right." She started to stand, but he was already there and, taking her hand, he helped her to her feet. Then he pulled her close and tenderly kissed her. "Bonsoir, *partner.*" He smiled at her. "Just for the record, there's no one I'd rather partner with in this little venture than you, Simone."

She nodded happily. "Me too. It's going to be fun."

"You go on up to bed, and I'll tend this fire and turn off the lights." He kissed her again. "Sleep well."

Simone went up to her sweet little room but suddenly felt wide awake. Whether it was the tea, the stimulating conversation, or happy thoughts of Kyle, she was not the least bit sleepy. She attempted to read awhile, but more awake than ever, she decided to sneak downstairs for a glass of milk. Sometimes that helped make her drowsy. Tiptoeing down the stairs, she was just passing through the foyer when the grandfather clock started to chime so loudly that she jumped in the air and fell against the tall antique. Holding onto its sturdy cabinet to steady it and herself, she waited for it to chime eleven times.

Then, about to release the solid base of the big old clock, her fingers ran over the ornately carved frontpiece. She'd admired this carving before — a beautiful depiction of trees, leaves, ferns, flowers, and birds —

but something about the front panel felt loose. Had she damaged it with her fall? She gently pushed the wood panel, hoping to nudge it back into place. But instead, it popped completely off. Worried she'd broken the valuable antique, she turned on a nearby lamp and bent down to examine it more closely — only to discover the panel had hidden hinges. It was a secret door.

She suddenly remembered her original mission — her search for her great-grandmamma's treasure. This was a good place to hide something very small. She moved the lamp close enough to see that, wedged in the tight space and barely showing, there was a strip of paper inside. Using her fingernails, she pried out an oversized yellowed envelope. With nervous fingers, she opened it. Whatever was inside, someone had taken great care to hide away.

But it was only a sepia-toned photograph of a very elegant elderly woman holding a baby in a lacy white gown and cap. She flipped it over, squinting to decipher the spidery writing on the back. *Simone Sophia von Hoffman Beaumont et Simone Sophia Beaumont. 20 juin, 1926.* She flipped it back over and stared in wonder. Based on the name and date, the infant in the photo could only be her great-grandmother, and the regal-looking older woman must be the baby's grandmother and, it seemed, her namesake. It was mind-boggling and yet strangely comforting in a solid, familial sort of way because the woman in the photo must also be Simone's ancestor — a grandmother from four generations back.

She stared at the photo with increased curiosity. The upward tilt of the older woman's chin, the styled waves in her hair, and her very elaborate jewelry . . . it all seemed to suggest something aristocratic . . . perhaps even royal. Was it possible that the Beaumont family roots were connected to some old European titled family? Or was Simone just fantasizing?

She studied the images of the jewelry more closely. This was not for everyday wear. Besides the ornate necklace and dangling sparkly earrings, the woman had on a tiara. Ladies of that era probably enjoyed wearing tiaras as a fashion statement, but something about this particular tiara suggested authenticity. The stones in these jewelry pieces were not small. She studied the woman's maiden name again, deciding that von Hoffman did not sound particularly French. Maybe Swiss or German or Austrian. But not French. It was all very intriguing.

She turned back to the photo, staring at those elegant jewels again. If those square cut, oval, and even heart-shaped gems were genuine — and she couldn't imagine that proud woman flaunting costume pieces — they would have to be extremely valuable. Although the photo wasn't in color, she guessed the white stones to be diamonds and the dark ones . . . emeralds, rubies, sapphires? But what had become of those pieces? Had they been passed down in the family? Perhaps even to Tante Estelle since she was the oldest living descendant in her family.

Simone focused on the sweet-faced baby in the lacy gown and wondered. Perhaps it was more likely that those pieces had been passed down to Simone Sophia's namesake, also the oldest girl in the Beaumont family? And if so, what had become of them? Her hand was trembling now. Was it possible that this was the treasure her great-grandmamma had written about? Was this what Simone was meant to find? But if that were true, where were the jewels hidden?

The sound of footsteps made her jump again, but it was only Kyle, descending the stairs with a sleepy expression. "Hey, what're you doing down here?"

"I wanted some milk — but never mind

that. You have to see this!" she whispered. Grabbing his hand, she tugged him into the library, turning on a table lamp. "I think I found the treasure."

"You're kidding!"

With her knees shaking in excitement, she handed him the photo, quickly explaining about the secret hiding place in the clock, then pointing out the names and date and her theory, impatiently waiting for him to examine the picture just as closely as she had. "Those have to be real jewels. And valuable ones. And the woman is obviously my great-grandmamma's grandmamma and namesake. But why has it been kept such a secret?"

"It's pretty mysterious, that's for sure."

"I know. And why was it so well hidden?"

"Apparently someone didn't want it found." He flipped it over again, staring with a furrowed brow. "Wow, those are some big old, hunking jewels. You sure they're not fakes?"

"In 1926? In Europe? And the way the old woman looks, do you think she'd wear fakes? I say they're real, and I bet they were supposed to be left to my great-grandmamma."

"That's a big assumption."

"Maybe. But it just makes sense. She's

the oldest girl. She's the namesake. She probably was supposed to get them when her grandmother passed away. Or perhaps she received them sooner. Maybe as an adult? She was eighteen when she left France. Maybe she already had them by then . . . but just didn't take them with her." Simone tried to imagine why someone would leave such valuable items behind.

"That's quite a theory, but let's go with it. If they were already in your great-grandmother's possession, why didn't she take them to America?"

"Maybe she forgot them in her rush to run away with her lover because she knew her father disapproved and they left suddenly. She didn't have time." She stared down at the photo that was still in his hands.

"I suppose that makes sense. But wouldn't she have sent for them later?"

"Yes. That's right. She said something to that effect in her letter. She did send for something, but I think they refused — or something like that —" She stopped at the sound of a throat clearing and turned to see Tante Estelle, in a blue quilted robe, standing in the doorway, her pale eyes filled with trouble.

Again, Simone explained how she found the photo. Saying how it was an accident.

211

Then she asked if Tante Estelle knew anything about it. At first her aunt acted surprised and as if she'd never seen the picture before. But then she sat down, and with a long weary sigh, confessed she did know about it.

"I put it there." She spoke slowly this time so Simone could understand. "You are right. That is my sister, Simone, with our grandmamma."

"Who was she to have such expensive jewels?" Simone asked.

"Our paternal grandmother. Simone Sophia von Hoffman was Austrian. The oldest daughter of a titled family. They escaped revolution by seeking refuge in Eastern France. Much was left behind. They brought what they could carry on wagons. Some wealth and jewels."

"These jewels?" Simone pointed to the photo.

"Oui. Simone Sophia von Hoffman married Grandpapa Beaumont. Their first son was my papa." Tante Estelle relayed all this information in a very weary monotone, as if painful to remember. Then slowly standing, she announced she was going to bed.

Not ready to let this mystery slip through her fingers, Simone eagerly asked what had become of the jewelry in the photo — could that possibly have been the treasure her great-grandmamma had mentioned in Simone's letter? "Wouldn't it have been very valuable?"

"Oui. Very valuable." Tante Estelle nodded.

"What happened to those jewels?" Simone repeated.

Without answering, Tante Estelle grasped her cane and limped toward the door.

Simone asked a third time, more urgently this time. "I know it probably doesn't seem important to you. It was so long ago. But I feel I must know. For my great-grandmamma's sake, I want to know the truth."

Tante Estelle turned to look at Simone and Kyle with sad eyes. "I took the jewels from my sister's jewelry box."

"The box upstairs? Above the armoire?"

Tante Estelle nodded. "My sister was gone. She left with the American flyer. I was angry and hurt. I deserved the family jewels, and Simone was dead to me."

"Your own sister was dead to you?" Simone couldn't grasp this.

"She stole my true love."

Simone slowly nodded. She'd suspected as much.

"I rescued the American. I nursed him

back to health. My sister stole him from me, so why should I not steal her inheritance? Which was more valuable? Cold hard jewels or a life?" Simone didn't know how to respond.

Tante Estelle shook her fist and speaking faster now, disparaged and cursed the selfish sister who betrayed and abandoned their family. "She broke Papa's heart!"

"And that made it right for you to take her jewels?" Simone asked.

Tante Estelle's eyes flashed with anger. "I did not do it at first. When my sister wrote to me from America, asking about her jewels, asking me to send them — I was shocked she'd left them behind. I told my papa. He gave me permission. He gave his blessing. He said to take the jewelry and to sell as I liked, so I used that money to purchase the clock and watch factory."

Tante Estelle sank into a chair near the door and let out a little sob. With downcast eyes, she continued to speak, rambling on as if unaware that anyone was still listening. She admitted that it had seemed right and fair and just at the time. Later on, she wasn't so sure. "Deceit drove a wedge between Simone and me. No more letters passed. The wall was built . . . and never came down."

"So that's the reason Great-grandmamma never spoke of her family in France, never wanted to come here." Simone shook her finger at the old woman. "Because of you! I can't believe you betrayed your own sister for a bunch of jewels."

Tante Estelle looked up with tear-filled eyes. "Je suis désolé," she apologized in a choked voice. "Je suis désolé." And then she stood up and hobbled away.

Simone, still trying to take the story all in, didn't know what to say or think. "So she did lie to me," she finally said to Kyle.

"How's that?" He frowned. "She just told you the truth."

"Not at first. And then she tricked me. She made me believe there might be a treasure here. She let us go all over the house and town and everywhere looking for it. All the while she knew she'd stolen it." Simone looked at him. "How can we trust her?"

He shrugged. "That happened a long time ago, Simone, and she seems sincerely sorry."

"But she stole my great-grandmamma's inheritance and then kept it secret. For all these years. And then from me."

"She did it to save the factory . . . people's jobs."

"But it was wrong." Simone shook the

photo. "She hid this because she knew it was wrong."

"She was young, and her father agreed it was okay. It had probably seemed right at the time. There was the war . . . deprivations . . . livelihoods. Tante Estelle did what she thought was best. You're probably just overly tired and overreacting —"

"I am *not* overreacting." She stepped away from him in anger. How dare he take Tante Estelle's side on this? What kind of business partnership were they entering into anyway? Maybe she'd been a fool to trust either of them. Tears of disappointment burned in her eyes and, still clutching the photo, she ran from the room and up the stairs . . . and eventually cried herself to sleep.

CHAPTER 16

Besides a throbbing headache, Simone felt foolish the next morning. Not because she'd trusted Tante Estelle and Kyle, but because she hadn't. She felt terrible for having been so accusatory last night. So unkind and ungracious. What had been wrong with her? Why had she gotten so upset over a bunch of old jewels? Was she that selfish?

Kyle had been right. She *had* overreacted. And now she regretted it. Sure, it had been wrong for her aunt to do what she'd done, but it had happened so long ago. And Tante Estelle had said she was sorry. Even the note in the old jewelry box had contained an apology. Simone had read it again this morning. *Je suis désolé.* They were three simple words, but seeing them there in the pink jewelry box seemed to confirm that Tante Estelle had truly regretted what she'd done. She had needed the money to save the clock and watch factory. Somehow

Simone had to repair this broken relationship with her aunt.

But when she went down for breakfast, Willa solemnly informed her that Estelle was feeling unwell this morning and had taken breakfast in her room. And Kyle had already eaten and gone into town for something. Feeling guilty for ruining Christmas Eve for everyone in the house, Simone didn't know what to do. And so she went up to her room and actually prayed for God's help and guidance. She had to make things right with Tante Estelle — as much for her own sake as for her great-grandmamma's.

Seeing it was close to ten, the time that her aunt usually had tea, Simone went downstairs and asked Willa if she could take it to her. Willa, busy with preparations for the evening festivities and not in the best frame of mind, begrudgingly agreed.

Simone felt uneasy as she carried the tray to Tante Estelle's bedroom. What if her aunt truly was ill? Possibly a reaction from Simone's bad manners last night. And what if she was unable to participate in Christmas because of this? Worse yet, what if she grew worse then died before Simone had a chance to make amends?

Tante Estelle, propped up by pillows in

her bed, looked small and frail and old . . . and very, very sad. Her eyes flickered with faint surprise when she realized it was Simone, not Willa, bringing her tea.

Simone simply set it on the side table then filled a cup, adding sugar and milk the way she knew her aunt liked it. She handed it to her with a weak smile. "Je suis désolé," she whispered.

Tante Estelle's gray brows arched as she set her teacup on the tray, asking Simone to repeat herself.

"Je suis désolé," Simone apologized again.

Tante Estelle's brow remained creased with confusion, as if she still hadn't heard correctly. She asked Simone why she was apologizing to her. Should not Estelle be apologizing to Simone?

Simone reached for her aunt's hand, explaining that she believed her great-grandmamma had sent her to Avre for a purpose that was far bigger than finding an earthly treasure. She had wanted Simone to repair her relationship with her younger sister. Great-grandmamma Simone Sophia had wanted to assure Estelle that all was well, all was forgiven. Simone solemnly told Tante Estelle that it was her dying wish.

Once again the woman's eyes filled with tears. But this time she held her arms out wide, and Simone went into them. With both of them hugging and crying and apologizing and expressing their love, they didn't even notice that Kyle had stepped into the bedroom. Standing by the side of the bed, he smiled down upon the happy reunion.

After they quieted down, Kyle took both Simone's and Tante Estelle's hands in his and, speaking slowly and clearly in French, he proclaimed that they had all found their treasure — a Christmas treasure that would last forever — love!

EPILOGUE

Exactly one year later, under the careful and creative management of Kyle and Simone, who both happily worked full time there, the Avre Clock and Watch Factory was fiscally recovered and profiting nicely. Jobs were secured, conditions improved, and the exterior of the building was even being historically restored. After a short tour of Europe, Kyle's mother, Katherine, fell in love with Avre and decided to make it her home too. But instead of retiring, she was now keeping books for the Avre Clock and Watch Factory.

It took less than two weeks for Cousin Sylvie to quit her position in the factory. She went to work for a cosmetics company in Cologne, but soon gave that up in order to marry Noel, assisting him in the hospitality industry. According to Marie, the happy couple was expecting, and she would be a grandmamma by summer.

Tante Estelle, enjoying excellent health due to her recently relieved conscience, was scheduled for hip replacement surgery after the New Year. In the meantime, she'd been making it to the factory twice a week and actively participating in decisions regarding the company's future. Her legacy would live on!

Kyle and Simone, engaged since last spring after a romantic picnic lunch in an Alpine meadow, had invited all their friends and family to fill the beautiful family church — midday on Christmas Eve. In a gown of old lace and creamy white satin, Simone was attended by her best friend, Andrea, who had taken much of the credit for how well Simone's trip to France had turned out. But as Simone walked down the aisle, she only had eyes for Kyle. Her groom looking incredibly handsome in his formal black suit. He looked even happier than she felt.

The newlyweds' plans for a honeymoon did not involve flying anywhere exotic but traveling by train to Paris where they looked forward to seeing the Parisian Christmas decorations together — for the first time. But before they boarded the train, Tante Estelle stepped away from the crowd of well-wishers in order to hand Simone an envelope, along with a kiss on the cheek.

Simone thanked her, then after getting settled in their seats, she opened the envelope to discover that Tante Estelle had legally assigned them ownership of her share of the Avre Clock and Watch Factory. Her note simply said: Mon trésor est ton trésor.

"My treasure is your treasure," Kyle translated the words that Simone already understood.

"Dear, sweet Tante Estelle." Simone slid the envelope into her purse then turned back to Kyle. And with snow flying, the train whistle blew. As the train pulled out of the station, the happy couple waved to family and friends standing on the platform . . . and turning back to each other, the happy newlyweds exchanged a nice long kiss. Yes, this would be a very good Christmas!

ABOUT THE AUTHOR

With around 250 books published and 7.5 million sold, **Melody Carlson** is one of the most prolific writers of our times. Writing primarily for women and teens, and in various genres, she has won numerous national awards — including the Rita, Gold Medallion, Carol Award, Christy, and two career achievement awards. Several of her novels have been optioned for film, and her first Hallmark movie, *All Summer Long,* premiered in 2019. Melody makes her home in the Pacific Northwest, where she lives with her husband near the Cascade Mountains. When not writing, Melody enjoys interior design, gardening, camping, and biking.